; OF

ls

SPEAKING OF
Journals

Children's Book
Writers Talk
About Their
Diaries, Notebooks
and Sketchbooks

Paula W. Graham

BOYDS MILLS PRESS

For R. J. G. —

Annam Carra. Soulmate always.

—*P. W. G.*

Text copyright © 1999 by Paula W. Graham

Published by Caroline House
Boyds Mills Press, Inc.
A Highlights Company
815 Church Street
Honesdale, Pennsylvania 18431
Printed in the United States of America

Publisher Cataloging-in-Publication Data
Graham, Paula W.
Speaking of journals : children's book writers talk about their diaries, notebooks, and sketchbooks / compiled by Paula W. Graham. —1st ed.
[240]p :. Ill. ; cm.
Summary: Children's book writers talk about their diaries, notebooks, and sketchbooks
ISBN 1-56397-741-9
1. Authors, American-Diaries-Authorship. 2. Creative writing. 3. Authorship. I. Title.
818/ .540308 20—dc21   1999   CIP
Library of Congress Catalog Card Number: 98-88261

First edition, 1999
Book designed by Charlotte Staub
The text of this book is set in Slimbach

10 9 8 7 6 5 4 3 2

Acknowledgments

ONE STORMY SUMMER DAY when the Atlantic surf at Dewey Beach, Delaware, was too dangerous for fishing or swimming, my Uncle Butch gathered my brother, sister, and me at his feet to read aloud his lost-at-sea journal.* From December 19, 1941, when Uncle Frank "Butch" Stewart's ship, the S. S. Prusa, was torpedoed by the Japanese, to January 19, 1942, when he reached the Gilbert Islands, my uncle survived aboard a lifeboat in the Pacific Ocean.

> Dec. 19, 1941. Torpedo struck aft near No. 5 hold 5:30 a.m. Ship sank in 9 min. Both lifeboats got away. 12 in one and 13 the other. 9 men lost.
> Dec. 20, 1941. Seas high, started leak. Sighted air patrol but he didn't see us.
> Dec. 25, 1941. Christmas very dull. 2 biscuits and 1/2 cup of water. Weather balmy and clear.
> Jan. 1, 1942. New Year's dinner extra cracker and water.
> Jan. 19, 1942. Sighted land 7:20 a.m. Reward $5 for first sight. Pulled an hour on oars for center of islands. Boat overturned in surf and hurt 2 men. All instruments of navigation saved.

As I sat listening to the brief entries about the second mate's funeral at sea, eager sharks butting against the bottom of the boat and the trial of a crew member caught stealing biscuits (they voted against throwing him overboard), my nine-year-old imagination created the scenes and seascapes to illustrate the stories. A career Merchant Marine, my uncle would have many other adventures at sea. Surviving the torpedo attack and the 2,200-mile trip from Honolulu to the Gilbert Islands aboard a lifeboat, convalescing

---

*"Log of Voyage Life Boat NO. 1 S. S. Prusa, 1941-1942 in Pacific Ocean" by Frank H. Stewart, C.W.T., USNR (unpublished journal)

under the care of the island priest, Father Claret, and eventually making his way home to Delaware on April 26, 1942: all were part of an adventure painful to revisit. Only once did he read aloud from this pocket-sized black leather book, but that was sufficient and I was hooked. For my tenth birthday my mother, Irene S. Whisenant, surprised me with a small book similar to Uncle Butch's. Emblazoned on the red plastic cover were the words Dear Diary. I was on my way.

Speaking of Journals, a book that simmered in the cauldron for three years, was seasoned by the many people who stirred, sipped, tasted, and tested along the way. For helping me create a blend of their stories, reflections and insights into the topic of journal keeping, I offer heartfelt thanks to

—all of the authors who interrupted writing schedules to talk to me in person or by telephone. I am grateful for your permission to print photos and excerpts from your personal journals.

—Kent L. Brown Jr. for his enthusiasm when this book was only an idea and to The Highlights Foundation Writers Workshop at Chautauqua, New York, which every summer gathers together aspiring writers and accomplished authors for a week of celebrating the art of writing for children. I was there in 1996. Part of the proceeds from the sale of this book will joyfully be donated to its scholarship fund.

—Jim Giblin, Marc Aronson, David Gale, Bill Hammond, Bill Sharp, Ann Angel, Larry Stoler, Libba Winston, Judie Simpson, Mary Frances Schneider, and Mary Arlene Hendricks, OSM, for contributing in your own unique ways.

—the following librarians for aiding with research and sources: Kathleen Horning at the Cooperative Children's Book Council, University of Wisconsin, Madison; Kris Adams Wendt, Rhine-lander (Wisconsin) District Library; Nancy Reidner, Mary Bloedow, Betty Cowin, and Jane Schimka of Rusk County (Wisconsin) Com-munity Library; Rob Reid, L. E. Phillips Memorial Public Library, Eau Claire, Wisconsin.

—booksellers and book lovers Blakely Beattey, Gail Waldron, and Phyllis Severud and Tammy Lundquist at the Blue Hills Bookseller in Rice Lake, Wisconsin, an oasis in the north woods.

And to my husband, Robert J. Graham, deepest thanks for creating a haven in the wilderness where dreams could bloom.

—*Paula W. Graham*

Contents

Preface

KEEPING A JOURNAL is living a wide-awake life. Whatever its name—notebook, sketchbook, log, daybook, diary, or journal—the blank book we fill with bits and pieces of our lives affirms us and validates our experiences. It also provides a safe place to make discoveries, celebrate one's story, and to confide, confer, question, and confess. Alert to the outside world, attuned to the inner one, the journal keeper lives with the consciousness that his or her life matters. Throughout history, as various strands of its traditions combined and recombined, the journal became an invention of writers, artists, naturalists, sea captains, and explorers. In the eighteenth century the journal served as a tool for self-education as men and women copied down in Commonplace Books observations, reflections, and pieces of wisdom from what they had read or otherwise experienced.

In recent years the journal has surfaced in American schools as a major component of the writing-across-the-curriculum movement. Teachers appreciate the connections between writing and learning, recognizing how writing clarifies thinking and helps to internalize new constructs. The classroom journal provides the workplace where students think about the relationship between themselves and the worlds of mathematics, literature, social studies, and science. In their journals children connect new strands of learning to what they already know. At the Columbia University Teacher's Writing Project, Lucy Calkins, author of *Living Between the Lines,* finds the notebook a lens through which children appreciate the richness that already exists in their lives.

Calkins and her colleagues discovered that writing in note-books not only changed the lives of their elementary school students, it also helped improve their writing skills. "Even if youngsters are just at the stage of beginning to collect bits of their lives, it's enormously helpful for them to have a farsight-ed vision of the role these entries might eventually play in cre-ating finished pieces of writing." In composition classes across grade levels, journals are a popular means of generating ideas, finding a focus, developing fluency, and experimenting with language. Authors Patricia Lee Gauch, Naomi Shihab Nye, and Kim Stafford were introduced to journal writing by their teach-ers. Pam Conrad, Kathleen Krull, Mary E. Lyons, and Eileen Spinelli received diaries as gifts. Jack Gantos pitched a fit on the kitchen floor until his mother gave him a diary like his older sis-ter's. Other writers had read or heard that keeping a journal was a good idea; some can't remember exactly how they got started. Many confess stumbling along, not knowing what they were supposed to write or how often.

Whether they carry journals in their shirt pocket, back pock-et, pocketbook or whether they write at home, all authors agree: the journal is a writer's laboratory. Marion Dane Bauer devel-oped her powerful writing skills by observing the world and exploring her emotions in the personal journal she began at age thirteen. For Bauer, who doesn't reread her journals, the very act of writing down is what imprints scenes on her brain. In *Writing Books for Young People,* James Giblin advises beginning writers to keep notebooks "to jot down ideas for new novels or picture books as they occur to you, or to write brief character sketches of two teenage girls you overhear on a bus or a little boy you see walking a big dog."

Not all writers keep journals. Katherine Paterson does not, nor do Chris Lynch, Tomie de Paola, Sharon Creech, or Lee Bennett Hopkins. Many others do, however, and the assortment of styles is illuminating and worthy of celebration. Madeleine L'Engle lives in her journal. In her "Everything Book" she records conversations with her family, friends, editors, and publishers. She copies quotes from other writers and reflects on them in writing. She records dreams, muses on topics like the unconscious and memory, and vents her grief and despair. A travel diary she kept on a ten-day trip to Portugal filled over 200 pages. Entire sections of her journal find their way into her published books.

Bruce Coville hammers out his frustrations on the computer keyboard. He then stuffs the printed pages into his private "Cranky Files," manila envelopes stored in a file cabinet. Historical fiction writer Mary E. Lyons enters into the life of her main characters by keeping personal journals in their first-person voices. Author and illustrator of award-winning nature books for young children Barbara Bash keeps three journals going at once: she takes a sketchbook into the field, writes personal material in another, and keeps a separate diary of her son's life. James Cross Giblin, a personal journal keeper for nearly forty years, now reflects on his professional life in a Writing Workbook. Poet Kim Stafford's faith in a fragment leads him to write small. In his hand-made Heart Pocket Books, Stafford captures wisps of life in a tiny journal he slips into his shirt pocket. Rich Wallace kept track of his mercurial teenage years in tiny books. Consulting them as a source for his writing transports him back into the emotions he experienced as a young man trying to find his place in the world. Picture book writer and poet David Harrison clips offbeat news items and files them randomly into idea folders. Between projects he sparks his imagination by exploring these folders.

In these ways contemporary children's authors continue the eclectic journal-keeping traditions of predecessors like Wanda Gag, Beatrix Potter, and L.M. Montgomery. When Wanda Gag started keeping a journal at age fifteen she listed her New Year's resolutions. For the next thirty years she carried a notebook wherever she went. She believed that keeping a diary as a young teenager gave her the courage later to explore her ideas in story

and picture book form. Beatrix Potter began her diary when she
was fourteen and never spoke to anyone about it. Found after
her death, the journal she kept until age thirty was written in
code. In it she catalogued the plants and animals she observed
in nature and recorded detailed descriptions of places she visited and pictures she saw in museums and galleries. Also found
among the bundle of loose pages were anecdotes gleaned from
newspapers.

L.M. Montgomery destroyed the childhood journals she began
in 1884 at age nine. Her surviving journals, which date from
1889 and continue to 1942, provided an outlet and safety valve
to release tension and boredom. Reared by stern maternal
grandparents on isolated Prince Edward Island, Montgomery
retreated to her journal to cope with loneliness, her wildly fluctuating emotions, and burgeoning creativity. When she turned
to writing for children she consulted her journals in order to
reenter the world of childhood and recreate its voice and
textures.

The authors interviewed for *Speaking of Journals* believe the
journal keeper should be free of rules. One doesn't have to write
in paragraphs or even complete sentences, one doesn't have to
record secrets, one doesn't have to write every day. Latitude is
limitless: sketching, writing, pasting things in. Everything goes:
ticket stubs, playbills, photographs, letters, copies of E-mail,
song lyrics, newspaper headlines. Stashing anything and everything into file folders, blank books, or manila envelopes counts
as journal keeping. Celebrating the creativity and diversity children's authors bring to their notebooks expands the possibilities
and gives us all permission to invent our own forms of journal
keeping.

Speaking of Journals is a collection of conversations with
contemporary authors who have written and/or illustrated
books for children. The poets, naturalists, and writers of fiction
and nonfiction interviewed for this book talk about why journal

keeping is an important part of their lives, how they got started, how their journal-keeping practices evolved, and how they currently use their notebooks. Also included are excerpts from childhood diaries as well as entries from current sketchbooks, notebooks, and journals. In a few cases authors have chosen to maintain privacy.

Barbara Bash

"One Hand, One Voice"

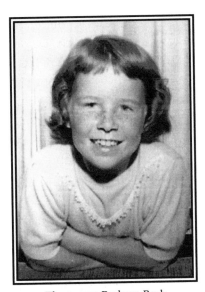

The young Barbara Bash

With sketchbook in hand Barbara Bash quiets the clamor of civilization and steps away from the demands of daily life. "Sometimes just picking up my journal, just holding it, leads me through a doorway and into another state of mind." Whether she's in the Arizona desert, under the canopy of an ancient Pacific Northwest forest, or on a river bank in India, Bash seeks out special places, opens her journal, and invites the natural world to speak to her.

By sitting quietly and listening and observing, Bash becomes part of the ecosystem. In her journal she weaves image and word, deepening her perceptions of the natural world and her connectedness to the creatures that inhabit it. With her pen she distills the spirit of place. What's true, what's alive, what's fresh filters through her consciousness and rests on the pages of her sketchbook. Back in her studio, Bash releases and refashions these spirits as she sets to work composing nature books for young children.

Bash first developed an interest in sketching the natural world when she lived at the edge of the Rocky Mountains. She credits Audrey Benedict—the Sierra Club author and naturalist who invited her to illustrate *A Naturalist's Guide to the Southern Rocky Mountains*—with stimulating her perceptions of the interconnectedness of life in an ecosystem. Benedict inspired Bash to do more than roam the tundra collecting specimens to bring back for botanical study. For the first time in her life Bash left the safety of her studio and stepped out into the elements. With majestic thunder clouds roiling far above her, she hunkered down to sketch moss campion and alpine flox, tiny plants that hug the earth.

The process of field sketching, of focusing on small things in a vast space, became as central to Bash as the finished product of her work. During the eleven years Bash spent in the field with Benedict, she learned that seeing is more than looking: it's holding the scene with all of the senses, relaxing into one's surroundings while remaining alert and expectant.

When field sketching, Bash sits waiting for secrets to be revealed. "I traveled to East Africa to sketch the baobab trees, to southern Colorado to watch the twilight emergence of 100,000 bats from an abandoned mine shaft, and to New York City to find birds' nests on skyscraper ledges. I watch and witness and draw. Words come to mind, settle on the page and complete the image."

Waiting beside the saguaro while researching *Desert Giant: The World of the Saguaro Cactus*, Bash witnessed the parade of creatures who make this cactus home: the gila woodpecker who taps out nesting holes, the tiny elf owl who moves into the moist, abandoned cactus interior, and Harris hawks who nest in the crooks of its spine-covered arms. Beneath a banyan tree in India, Bash discovered a shady crossroads of village life, a place where villagers come to worship, barter, rest, and share stories, while high in its branches owls, monkeys, and bats conduct their own affairs.

Field sketching has led Bash to the lives of long-nosed bats, curved-billed thrashers, javelina pigs, and stripe-tailed scorpions. A sketchbook experience in India, where she spent two months researching *In the Heart of the Village: The World of the Indian Banyan Tree,* impressed on her the importance of establishing connections with people before drawing them. Fascinated by women washing clothes on the steps of the river, Bash quickly set to work sketching them. She was immersed in her work when a woman began yelling and pointing at her. Startled, Bash was flooded by a wave of vulnerability: she was in a foreign culture unable to speak the language, being chastised by other women. "It taught me about making a relationship with people before I sketch them, about learning their words for 'is it OK if I draw you?'"

As children experience the tumult and pressures of the world, Barbara Bash's work offers them a nurturing alternative. Upon opening her stunning nature books, the reader follows Bash into sacred spaces, each page a tapestry of richly textured images and distilled prose. This artist/writer who weaves beauty and insight proves that the natural world offers countless treasures worth celebrating.

Barbara Bash's books include

Shadows of Night: The Hidden World of the Little Brown Bat
Urban Roosts: Where Birds Nest in the City
Ancient Ones: The World of the Old-Growth Douglas Fir
Desert Giant: The World of the Saguaro Cactus
Tree of Life: The World of the African Baobab
In the Heart of the Village: The World of the Indian Banyan Tree

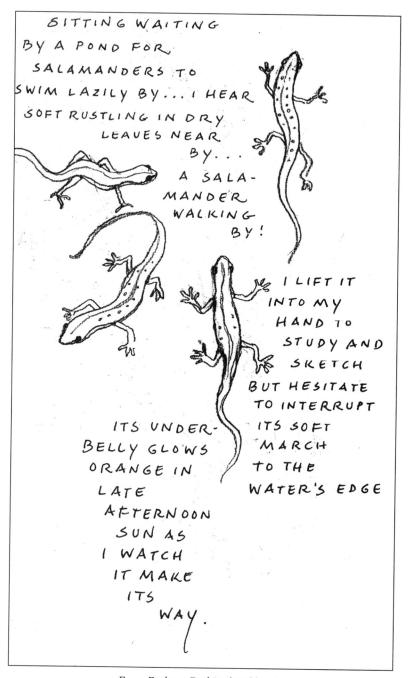

SITTING WAITING
BY A POND FOR
SALAMANDERS TO
SWIM LAZILY BY... I HEAR
SOFT RUSTLING IN DRY
LEAVES NEAR
BY...
A SALA-
MANDER
WALKING
BY!

I LIFT IT
INTO MY
HAND TO
STUDY AND
SKETCH
BUT HESITATE
TO INTERRUPT
ITS SOFT
MARCH
TO THE
WATER'S EDGE

ITS UNDER-
BELLY GLOWS
ORANGE IN
LATE
AFTERNOON
SUN AS
I WATCH
IT MAKE
ITS
WAY.

From Barbara Bash's sketchbook

The Interview

I've always loved the experience of handwriting. As a toddler I would fill up page after page with illegible writing. I think that was the beginning of my love of the act of writing. This led to my fascination with the alphabet and calligraphy and eventually the making of books.

As a teenager I found the drawing of letters to be a wonderful creative outlet. I spent many high school math classes filling up the margins of mimeographed work sheets with letterforms. The images I worked with in art classes usually had the name of the object, or a quote related to it, integrated into the design. The letters and words were as alive an expression to me as the painting. I pored over Ben Shahn's book, *Love and Joy About Letters*, fascinated with the bold way he combined words and images.

After college I dove deeply into the study of calligraphy and made my living for many years as a calligraphic designer. During this period I began to reconnect with drawing—which was surprisingly easy to do because that part of my brain had been working all along drawing the calligraphic line.

This reconnection to drawing was nurtured through my study of nature and my relationships with naturalists. I began working with Audrey Benedict when she was writing a book on the Southern Rocky Mountains for the Sierra Club. She asked me to illustrate it. It took us eleven years to finish the book, and during the course of that time we made several trips into the field. She opened my eyes to the interconnectedness in nature. I also began to trust the importance of sketching outdoors on our trips together. It was a heady experience of learning to relax out in the elements and stay focused.

Combining Word and Image

Combining word and image in my journal is a particular kind of gathering together that's really important to me. I go out into an ecosystem and draw. By drawing it, I know it in a more intimate way. Even if it seems much too complicated to capture on the page, when I try to draw it I make an inner connection and understand it in a physical way.

The writing that goes in around those sketches is a simple personal response to a place—what my senses are taking in. These observations become a springboard for writing about a particular ecosystem. My sketchbook holds my particular impressions of the real place.

Combining drawing and writing brings out a different quality of my mind. I sketch something, then comment on it, and the comments are sometimes very surprising. The drawing puts me into a contemplative state of mind—that's just the nature of drawing. You have to be there to do it—it's the physics of the act. Because my mind is present, the words that come out have a kind of freshness that I find sweet and inspiring.

It was when I began my first children's book, *Desert Giant: The World of the Saguaro Cactus,* that drawing and writing came together and my journal emerged as a source book for my professional life. Because I came to the process of writing for children from a visual perspective, I thought I was going to have someone else write *Desert Giant.* But when I came back from being in the desert I knew so much about the saguaro that I thought, "This is crazy. I am just going to have to explain all of this to someone else." So I decided to sit down and tell the story myself.

I began with a series of drawings. I just sat there and looked at my drawings, then started to write the story. Having the words come out in response to the sketches was an organic process. Now I love making books where it's my pictures and words coming together. It's one hand, one voice.

Field Sketching

When I'm working on a book my experience of going out into the field is focused. With *Desert Giant* I had come up with the idea of showing a tree as the center of an ecosystem, rooted in place and providing nourishment and protection. It seemed to be a natural visual focus, with a wonderful sense of sacredness coming through between the lines. So I looked through books, searching for which tree to study. When I read that the saguaro cactus was pollinated by long-nosed bats, something wondrous captured my mind and drew me in.

So, first I get hooked by the subject, then I go to the place and see for myself. I wander around and then sit down and draw. I focus on the tree itself and then I get curious about who the other players are. While I may have prepared myself some-what—this bird may show up, or that lizard—I don't know what's going to happen. I love seeing who appears—watching the place reveal itself. This can happen, I believe, because I am sitting still and drawing for long periods. The rhythm of the ecosystem emerges in this quiet space.

Audience, Honesty, and Privacy

My journal is the way I keep connected with my particular experience of the world. Sometimes I feel like I'm so easily influenced and sensitive to other people's perceptions of things, but this is the place where it's just me and my thoughts and my feelings.

Right now I have three different tracks going in my journal keeping. I have the field sketch books, which are good to share with the world. Most of my field sketching feeds into published work, perhaps eighty percent. Then I also have times when I'm just outdoors recording my experience in an open, unfocused way. My journal keeping goes in surges. When I'm in my studio, all of my energy goes into the final art. When I've finished a book, I'll get back into the field with my journal in hand.

I also have a diary that I started keeping for my son when he was born. It's filled with "you did this" type entries. Then there is the journal where I express moments of confusion. I don't write in it when I'm happy, so it's just a book of painful moments. I find it helpful to review it every so often because it gives me perspective. Maybe I'm no longer struggling with something; maybe I'm cycling through the same old internal battle again.

I'm interested in creating a journal where I integrate the feelings that are safe to express with the ones that tend to be hidden away. I'm intrigued with the relationship between these two, bringing together my field sketching notebook with more of the inner workings of my private journal. I'll always need a place where I can put certain feelings that would be better buried and left to decompose. I've taken some solitary retreats recently where I've begun to create this deeper field journal voice. This is new territory for me—a joining of the public and private selves. Can they meet in my sketchbook? Intimacy can be so deep and yet so simple.

Journal Companions

I enjoy reading the journals of other writers and naturalists—May Sarton and Anne Lamott and Terry Tempest Williams, for example. A few years ago I discovered the field sketch books of Claire Walker Leslie. Her books have been very helpful in my field sketching classes, full of good suggestions and drawing examples that are not so perfect as to be unattainable to the beginner. I also recently discovered a book of journal writing by Chris Ferris called *The Darkness is Light Enough—Field Journal of a Night Naturalist.* This book has affected me deeply in its description of the comfortable relationship she developed with the natural world at night.

Journal as Doorway

Sometimes just picking up my journal, just holding it, leads me through a doorway and into another state of mind. Often I resist going through the doorway. But the moment I've got my journal in hand and step into that other place, I'm happy. To look at something closely, to be curious about the world, always lightens things up for me.

There's something about the attempt to draw that makes the difference. It can be hard to talk ourselves out of that controlling voice that judges the marks we make. When I get back home from drawing and flip through my sketchbook, I'm always surprised that my drawings look as good as they do. The real work is quieting that voice that says, "I can't do it," and just getting down to observing, drawing, and learning. I end up surprising myself.

An interesting place for me to draw is the zoo, where so many animals are close enough to observe. I sit in one place and the creature begins to relax a little with me. There is a natural process of observing, getting comfortable with the animal and then starting to record its movements. As I sketch, people will come by, look at my drawings, make a comment, then move on. After a while the animal notices that I am still sitting there. I love that moment of attention.

David Harrison

"Keeping a Life"

David Harrison as a boy

A peek at David Harrison's early journals reveals a boy skipping across an alfalfa field, butterfly net in hand, trailing painted ladies, buckeyes, cabbage and sulphur butterflies. Reading between the lines, one sees him hard at work observing, recording, and caring for his butterfly and moth collection. On September 16, 1952, he makes plans to rewrite the labels for his 230 butterflies and create record cards for each of the 150 species. On April 28, 1957, he catches a butterfly unlike any he has ever seen: "a large white butterfly slightly tinted green." On August 22, 1957, he takes all of his insects out of their cellophane envelopes to air them. He fears the high humidity is making them moldy.

As a child Harrison also collected stamps, coins, fossils, arrowheads, snakes, seashells, animal skins, birds' nests, and skulls—anything he could sneak into the house past his mother. Forty plus years later he is still collecting. Where he once recorded butterfly data in compact spiral notebooks, he now uses file folders to collect anything that catches his fancy: facts, ideas, and anecdotes. He scribbles a note to himself: "Temperatures rise with the depth of a mine shaft, but fall in a cave. Key clue in mystery?"

In the 1975 *Guinness Book of World Records* Harrison reads of Robert Pershing Wadlow of Alton, Illinois, the tallest man on record who at the age of 22 reached a height of 8 feet, 11.1 inches. Robert's shoe size was 37AA. Harrison types notes about Robert Wadlow for his clipping file.

Guinness entries about other unusual people also make it into Harrison's file folders. Jozef "Count" Boruslaski, born November 1739 in Poland, measured 8 inches at birth, 25 inches at age 15, and 39 inches at age 30. The lightest human adult was Lucia Zarate of Mexico who weighed 4.7 pounds at age 17.

From newspapers Harrison has assembled a collage of offbeat animal stories: pachyderms on the loose, a kangaroo resisting arrest by two Chicago policemen who tried to handcuff it, and mice hooked on marijuana. There's the story about the toll taker at the Florida Turnpike's Jupiter exit who shares the night shift with an owl that perches on an ultraviolet lamp and swoops down on bugs. And the one about Nan La La, the crawfish who was disqualified from all future appearances in Texas crawfish races because someone doctored his tail with hot sauce. These tidbits of fact and fancy germinate in Harrison's idea file until he is ready to give them flight in picture books and poetry.

He can't throw anything away. Even ancient yellowing contributions and curling photos still claim a rightful place in Harrison's idea file. When he's in search of a project, this collection of manila folders—fat with bits and pieces, odds and ends—is the archaeological site he visits.

Everything Harrison keeps serves as a reminder of what he has done and where he has been, possible preludes to his future writing. A journal entry pulls him back instantly to boyhood with worries of gangly knees and heavy glasses that kept sliding down his nose. A cartoon about cows standing in a field, visiting, starts him wondering if cows have secret lives and inspires the rhyming picture book *When Cows Come Home*. Until he needs them, his treasury of random thoughts, newspaper clippings, magazine articles, and cartoons remains tucked away in the idea file.

Harrison also draws on his eclectic life experience. By the time he was 21, Harrison had worked in a pet shop, taught music, dug ditches, unloaded boxcars, played in dance bands, poured concrete, and explored caves. He has been a principal trombonist in the Springfield (Missouri) Symphony, a pharmacologist in Mead Johnson Research Laboratory, editorial manager for Hallmark Cards, and a businessman.

In 1969, when Harrison was serving as children's greeting card editor at Hallmark Cards and writing short stories for the adult market, a colleague expressed surprise that he wasn't writing for children. Accepting the challenge, he wrote *Boy With a Drum*. He confesses to being so smitten by the experience that he decided to do it again. Today, more than forty titles later, Harrison's work has been translated into nine languages, distributed in thirteen countries, and sold more than fifteen million copies.

Since childhood David Harrison has been too busy living life to set aside a regular time to record his thoughts and feelings. For him, sporadic journal keeping is the only practical way to do it, and while half the value is in making a journal, the other half is in saving it and utlilizing its contents in his writing. He stores his boyhood notebook in a drawer by the desk where he writes.

Harrison sides with the pack rats of the world who save, value, and stash away everything that might come in handy. The result: David Harrison's whimsical poetry and magical books that germinate in idea files, flutter through his imagination, and delight the fancy of readers around the world.

David Harrison's books include

The Boy with the Drum
Somebody Catch My Homework
The Purchase of Small Secrets
When Cows Come Home
The Book of Giant Stories
Poetry for the Fun of It (for adults)

The Interview

When I was twelve or thirteen years old I began recording information that was important to me. I was a nutty zoologist, though I wouldn't have called myself that. I loved nature, and I brought as much of it inside, into my bedroom, as my mother would allow: birds' nests, butterflies, snake skins, funny-looking rocks, fossils, arrowheads, the wings from dead birds, and sea shells when we went on trips.

I identified strongly with my collections. I became quite involved in learning the Latin names and going to the library and checking to see what I had just captured or found. I was meticulous about dusting and washing and polishing and labeling. I took secret pride in seeing adults' eyes widen when I gave them some fourteen-syllable Latin name for a common butterfly.

During that period, I was probably best known for my butterfly collection. I spent so much time in the field collecting that I began to record many of those observations in a little, inexpensive, three-ring leather-bound spiral notebook. I have it in a drawer by my desk where I write today, and from time to time I pull it out and look at it.

The significance of my journal is that it leads me back instantly to who I was. I can become that twelve-year-old kid again, worry about his complexion and his glasses that were heavy and kept sliding down his nose when he was hot, getting gangly with big feet and knees. Then there was my father who was not at all certain that it was a manly thing for his son to be doing, running around in the neighbor's field with a butterfly net. As such memories flood back to me they in turn generate other thoughts and patterns of thinking.

I treasure those childlike observations that I made so many years ago. Making a journal is valuable, but saving it is equally important. Those events in my youth helped shape me as an adult. Looking at my journal gives me a way to get in touch with myself in an earlier time.

Sporadic Record Keeping

That was the only time I ever kept a formal written record. In my college years I had absolutely no time in my life to devote to any kind of journal keeping. I was one of those kids who was busy when I was little and I grew up that way. By the time I went through four years of college, I had activities every night: fraternity meetings on Monday nights and symphony rehearsal on Tuesday nights; DeMolay meetings on Wednesdays and choir rehearsal on Thursdays; bowling on Friday nights. I gave music lessons from 7:30 a.m. on Saturday until 6:00 that evening. I would play in a dance band Saturday night, sing in the choir on Sunday, and direct the choir on Sunday evening.

I was living my life, but I sure didn't have time to write about it. I was twenty-one years old and about to graduate from Drury College when I rediscovered writing. At that point it had been many years since I had written anything in a diary or in journal form.

Some people are faithful to their journals or diaries, and if you happen to be like that, good for you. If you feel comfortable setting aside a regular time to record your thoughts, fine. It doesn't work for everyone. Many of us tend to write only when the mood strikes or when we meet someone interesting or perhaps go on a trip.

Sporadic record keeping certainly has value, and it's probably

From David Harrison's journal

more likely to get done if people don't feel guilty about not doing it in the meantime. For someone like me it's the only practical way to do it. Once when I went to England to research a book, I kept meticulous notes, all day, every day, wherever I was. I would stop at a forest that was just exploding with blossoms, blue bells and ferns as far as I could see. I snapped pictures, tape-recorded cuckoo birds in trees, recorded my impressions, and wrote notes.

I came back with two hundred pages of handwritten notes of my three weeks in England—going through the ruins of an old castle, sitting on the slopes leading to the castle with the wind in my hair, listening to ravens croaking along below me. All of those experiences and observations were important so I wrote them down. Experimenting with journal keeping on a trip is a good way to get into it. It's certainly a good way to write out an emotional crisis, too—the death of someone dear, the loss of a pet, moving away. Once we develop the habit of keeping some sort of record, entries may tend to come closer together over time, but even when it's six months or a year between dates, that doesn't mean that we've stopped.

My tendency these days is to jot down ideas in the car with one hand, which is a terrible habit. Not only that, I can't read it later. I've begun using a small tape recorder instead so that I can transcribe the notes later. I especially find that helpful when I'm contemplating a longer piece or subject that will need a lot of structure and organization.

Clipping File: Ideas, Nuggets, and Thoughts

Those early notebook observations are what I consider my only real, authentic journal entries in the traditional sense. What I have done most of my writing career has been fill folders with notes, ideas, and clippings. I have a *Far Side* calender on my desk, which is as much a part of my furniture as the clock. If somebody doesn't get me one for Christmas I march out to get one for myself. I only turn one page a day, because that's the way I start my morning. From time to time I save one that I especially like for the idea folder. A recent example shows a *Tyrannosaurus rex* reading his calendar. In every square on his Jurassic calender it says, "Kill something, eat it. Kill something, eat it. Kill something, eat it." I have no idea how I would ever find a use for such an idea, but into the file it went.

The impulse for *When Cows Come Home* originated from a cartoon. It showed cows standing in the field, visiting. When a car approached they grazed until it was safe to stand up again and resume their chatting. I began speculating about the possibilities if cows really have secret lives. Three or four years later that notion had germinated enough to become *When Cows Come Home*.

There is a newspaper article in my idea file about a woman in

Wichita who saw a hippopotamus standing by the road as she drove home from a luncheon. No one believed her. Her husband wondered if she'd been overly served. Her thirteen-year-old daughter was downright skeptical.

In desperation she called the sheriff's office and learned there had been a road show passing by Wichita the night before and had stopped to water the big animals. In the dark a baby hippopotamus slipped into a pond and escaped. That article became the basis for a picture book story, *Monster, Monster.*

My idea file, a series of manila folders, is fat with bits and pieces and odds and ends. It's not organized. Some of the ideas go back to when I was writing stories for adults. It's like an archaeological dig when I go through it from time to time. The oldest contributions are looking pretty ancient and yellow. But if I try to throw them away—and can't—I know that they still have a rightful place in the file.

I found a note in there recently that informed me that in a cave the temperature stays essentially the same no matter how deep or how far you go into it, whereas in a mine shaft, it gets hotter the deeper you go. If that's true it would make a good clue if I ever wrote a mystery in which someone is blindfolded and kidnapped and whisked away into some underground hiding place.

Another note, scribbled on a scrap of paper: "I wonder if dirt'll hurt a turtle?" Sounds a little saucy. Probably wouldn't use it. But it's in here.

I'm most likely to dig through the file when I'm in search of a project. Until I need them, it's a good place to tuck ideas away.

A Life of Their Own

Ideas, observations, clippings, photos, etc. can be kept in many formats. Scrapbooks, for example, photo albums from vacations. Magazine articles of special interest. Anything I hang on to serves as a reminder of something I've done, something that's happened, something that someone I know or have heard about has done: a poem by Robert Frost, a quotation by Einstein.

Not long ago I found in one of the folders several descriptions of trees by different authors. Milne saw a tree just the thing for his bear to climb when looking for honey. Joyce Kilmer thought it a wondrous creation of God, and Hemingway found trees useful as a canopy over the beginning of his great love story. I suppose I was thinking about how many ways there are to express ourselves and to see and describe our subjects. Maybe the next time I run across that little collection of tree descriptions, some other thought will beam to mind. It seems to serve as a stimulator for thinking. I don't know, maybe the pack rats of the world are right: If you think that something is important enough to keep, put it away and hang on to it. Somewhere down the line maybe it will stimulate you to see, think, or express yourself differently.

Keeping a Scrapbook

My mother is the scrapbook maker in our family. Recently she spent months updating all the scrapbooks and she presented me with several of them, a magnificent gift representing a lifetime of loyal support. Talk about a fantastic present—all these pictures with captions of who this was and what we were doing—and now I will always have these. The first one is preschool years, the second is elementary school, the next one is high school, then college. There's one of my young adulthood and finally one filled with clippings about my years as a writer. She also made scrapbooks for our son, our daughter, and my sister. I've already dived into my elementary scrapbook to write a poem about my first day of school.

Keeping Correspondence

I'm a keeper of correspondence and copies of my answers to people, which also helps me get back to particular events or incidents. Several years ago, along with thirty of my manuscripts, I gave fourteen hundred letters to the Ward Edward's Library in Warrensburg, Missouri. Several more files have accumulated since then.

Connecting Life and Art

Not long ago I spent time going through collections of files and scrapbooks. I was looking for ways to remember my childhood from ages five to ten. I was able to make a list that included the first day of school, when I was chosen to lead the rhythm band, when the big boys beat the snot out of me, when my mother found a dead lizard under my pillow and thought it was a scorpion, when I went to see *The Mummy's Tomb* and was afraid to be left alone for a week. And many more, some fifty in all, most of which will probably become poetry for a manuscript I'm writing about my early life.

Poetry requires honesty, and if I'm writing about my early life it's important to me to set it down the way it was. I had a great childhood, but I needed to rediscover times and events that weren't so happy in order to present a truthful and complete picture. For one year and a half, my parents and I lived in a crude little house. Not because we were so destitute, but because when we moved back from Ajo, Arizona, to Springfield, Missouri, in 1945, World War II had just ended, and with everybody coming home from the service, housing was nonexistent.

The only place we could find to rent was on the farm of a family who raised show horses. They neglected their own home, but their horse barn was magnificent. While carpenters built the barn, they lived in a tiny, two-room building with a concrete floor. By the time we rented it, a glassed-in porch had been added across the front. We heated with a coal stove and visited the privy out back. I tend to forget that water could freeze in glasses on especially cold winter nights and that sometimes we slept in our clothes and piled coats on top of the covers. To me that wasn't an unhappy time. I made some friends, learned how to ride horses, and shot my first bow and arrow. Conditions at times were miserable, but we weren't down and out about it. Both of my parents were positive people, so I grew up the same way.

For the most part I enjoyed being a kid and it gives me pleasure to share my thoughts and reminiscences with young people. I used to tell my parents that if they'd really loved me they would have given me a rotten childhood so that I could grow up and become famous writing about it.

Jennifer Owings Dewey

"My Home Away from Home"

Jennifer Owings Dewey, age 4

Jennifer Owings Dewey began keeping a journal at the age of eight and found between its covers a place to nurture her secret life as writer and illustrator. Frequently unsupervised as a child and facing numerous family difficulties, Dewey roamed the desert landscape of northern New Mexico on her pony Babe with pet pig Jerome in tow. It never occurred to her to feel frightened. So attached was Dewey to the outdoors, she carried around the feeling that if she ever needed to escape her lot, she could do so as a wild animal.

Completely at home in deserts and mountains where she retreats to settle her mind, Dewey's constant companion is her

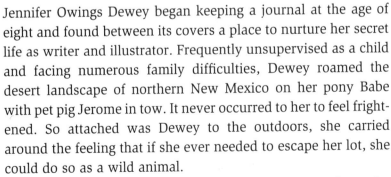

journal. As both an illustrator and an author, she first captures experiences in sketches, then surrounds them with a few vivid words, a process she compares to writing haiku. She listens to the language of landscape, wind, and silence. By sketching and writing about the sounds of nature, the movement of animals, and the way the ground feels to her feet, Dewey merges with her environment. These details, transformed by pencils and crayons, later become clues and reference points for her children's books.

Dewey's work is a blend of scientific fact and personal experience. She begins *Rattlesnake Dance* with a true story of being bitten by a rattlesnake when she was nine years old. Riding Babe alone in the hills north of her family's New Mexico ranch, Dewey stopped to climb the face of a sandstone ridge. Reaching over the ledge she interrupted the nap of a prairie rattlesnake. The story of the strike, her trip to the hospital, and her recovery is interspersed with rattlesnake lore, Indian legends, and scientific facts. Then follow two stories of rattlesnake events—a Hopi rain ceremony and rattlesnake dance—also based on first-hand experience.

No longer private, but still safe, Dewey's journals trigger new book ideas. She opens her journal, flips through the pages, and begins making notes. New ideas always speak to her. Once when Dewey was backpacking in Colorado, she met a young Navajo girl. The daughter of sheepherders, the girl was feral— lovely, happy, well-adjusted, but very wild. This chance meeting is incubating in her mind and in her journal, the genesis of a story about a child who runs off and finds her way back to civilization. Dewey will use another journal to develop this story line. She feels safe, because nobody is looking over her shoulder, ready to criticize should she mess up or hit a dead end.

The pattern of taking personal experience from her journal and crafting it into stories and books has also resulted in "Jennifer's Journal," a regular feature in *Highlights for Children* magazine.

Another recent nonfiction book, *Mud Matters: Stories from a Mud Lover*, with photographs by Stephen Trimble, combines personal experience with facts; it's a collection of stories concerning the author's relationship to mud.

More recently Dewey tapped childhood memories to write *Navajo Summer*, an autobiographical novel for children about her life with a Navajo family on a reservation in Arizona. As they explored Canyon de Chelly, a sacred place to the Navajos, Dewey sketched the ruins and rock art, intuiting at age twelve and thirteen that she would end up writing about it some day.

Dewey's interest in teaching journal writing has taken her into urban environments. In the summer of 1997 when she taught "Understanding Nature Through Drawing and Writing" to a group of elementary teachers in Baltimore, a question by the director—"do you know how to get here?"—prompted Dewey to begin a book for children about finding one's way when lost. It will be a combination of stories from her journal and interviews with people who navigate rivers and track the forests. It will contain useful information about how to make a connection with urban, rural, or wilderness environments.

As Dewey writes and illustrates this work-in-progress, she will sit down, read through her journals, and remember the day on the glacier, hours by the river, or the time her vehicle broke down in the desert and, short on water, she needed to find her way back. Any of these experiences in the natural world, recorded in her journals, will suggest narrative threads for this book, as well as Dewey's future projects.

Jennifer Owings Dewey's books include

Rattlesnake Dance: True Tales, Mysteries and Rattlesnake Ceremonies
Wildlife Rescue: The Work of Dr. Kathleen Ramsay
Navajo Summer
Family Ties: Raising Wild Babies
Bedbugs in our House
Mud Matters: Stories from a Mud Lover

The Interview

I was eight years old when I started keeping journals. One of the things that was mine and belonged to me alone was the little book where I recorded words and pictures about things that were going on. I had a difficult childhood. I used to write poetry and I was shy about it so I kept it private. The journal was my secret life as poet and illustrator. I realized that I could write whatever I wanted, not just poetry, because the journal was mine and no one was going to say, "Oh, you can't think that, you can't write that."

Home Away from Home

I love the experience of keeping a journal. I get pleasure from recording and documenting interesting and beautiful experiences. As an illustrator and an author, I tend to draw a lot of pictures in my journals. By combining pictures and words I climb right into an experience, with no barriers between me and whatever I'm experiencing. In all of my travels, and I do a lot of this, my journal is where I create a home away from home. Drawing a new environment makes me feel closer to it, less afraid or nervous. I never worry about grammar, punctuation, or spelling when writing in my journal. I try to get the image with the pictures so I know what I saw, but it's always impressionistic, never an exact replica.

Making the Unfamiliar More Familiar

When I was a kid, I wrote to create order out of the chaos of a troubled family. Now it's to make the unfamiliar more familiar. Recently I went on a wilderness river trip in the Utah canyons. There were three young children along. I was their designated entertainer. I'd brought journals and various art supplies for each of them. In the canyons we encountered the most extraordinary beetles. At first the kids were horrified. But I convinced them to draw the beetles. We got down on our hands and knees and watched them walk. We drew them from ground level. At the end of the trip we found a huge white spider—an albino tarantula—swimming in the water. Instead of being afraid, the kids couldn't wait to camp so they could pull out their pencils and sketchbooks and draw the odd animals. One reason I keep a journal is to allow for this kind of experience.

Materials

I feel like a spoiled brat when I go to the art store to buy my supplies because I love to get expensive paper and pencils. And I'm only going to get exactly what I want. There's something about the feel of paper and the quality of the line that for me has to be a certain way or it doesn't work. For me, I can't stand paper you see through. Ball point pens just don't make it for me. I love leather-bound journals, the "real" thing.

Fieldwork

When I'm working in an ecosystem I start with the pictures. I have tremendous respect for what comes off my mind and

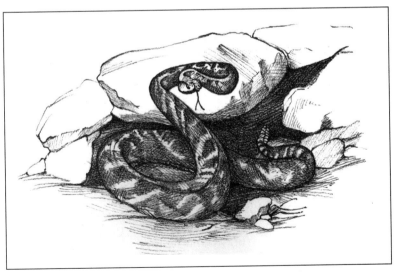

From Jennifer Owings Dewey's sketchbook

heart in the experience of drawing, so I don't work it too much. I try to keep the spontaneity, the original impressions. When it comes to the words, it's almost like haiku. I write down a few select, descriptive words, which are clues and reference points for the narrative I'm going to write. If I'm in the desert, for example, I'll write down three words about a cactus. I never consciously think that I'll move those words into the text of a book, but they are markers to take me back to the experience when I fill out the narrative later.

Part of what I do in my journals is listen to the language of the landscape, which includes listening to animal sounds, the wind, even silence. For me, the purpose of going out into the wilderness with my journal is to learn the language and geography of the physical world. Sketching and writing about every level of the experience—the way the ground feels on my feet, the way the birds move in the sky, the sounds they make—helps me know, and later remember, what's happening out there.

Constant Companion

There is a kind of regularity about my journal keeping, but it depends on how my work is going. When I'm researching in the field I may spend an entire morning with my journal. When I'm at home working on the drawing board or writing a book, I use the late afternoon for sitting with my journal. Sometimes when I'm spending six or seven hours per day on a manuscript, I won't be able to open my journal until I take some free time on the weekend. I love to go off into the mountains on the weekends to draw and write in my journal.

My Life Is an Open Book

At this point in my life I have close to thirty journals. Unfortunately I don't have my childhood journals because I was sent off to boarding school when my parents split up and my mother took all of my stuff to Goodwill. When I came home for my first Christmas all of my belongings, including my journals,

Capturing a slice of nature

were gone. It was years before I recovered from losing them.

When my own children were growing up I'd record a lot of their experiences in my journals. As they've grown, they've asked for these because they want to read about themselves and see pictures of themselves when they were little. I gladly give them these journals. But if I have material I plan to tap for books, I hold on to it. I look back into a journal if I get bogged down. By rereading I remind myself of the direction I wanted to take.

Words of Wisdom

I noticed how the three children on the river trip loved having their own journals and pencil boxes. We worked out at the beginning that the children could go to their backpacks and pick out what they wanted anytime they wanted it. They didn't have to go through the ritual of asking an adult's permission.

A journal is a place where you can create whatever you wish and not worry about anything. At first these kids, aged four, six, and eight, felt as if they had to ask, "Is it OK if I use a black pencil for this red bug?" "Is it OK?" came up a million times. I finally sat them down and said, "Let's pretend today that we're not going to say 'Is it OK?' even once." It worked. They looked at me. I could see the words forming on their lips. They would stop and swallow them.

I think it is necessary for parents to make a conscious effort to take children out into a less-civilized environment, even if it's just going to a park to watch birds in a pond. Something as simple as that will open a person's mind to the freedom to think about things in a new way. Because the lives of so many children are urban and controlled, the wilderness seems a big scary place. If children can be introduced to the outdoors in increments, the chances are that their fears will dissolve. If they come to journal writing with a sense of a larger world, they will express themselves there, on those pages, their very own pages.

Eileen Spinelli

"Life's Small Moments"

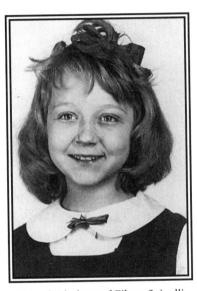

Schoolgirl photo of Eileen Spinelli

From the time she was a little girl, Eileen Spinelli knew she wanted to be a writer. When her second grade teacher, Miss Campbell, read one of her compositions aloud as an example of bad writing, Spinelli remembers receiving her first big rejection. In response to Miss Campbell's assignment to write an essay about food, Spinelli had composed a fictional account of a royal wedding feast. But public humiliation by Miss Campbell did not deter Spinelli. She was so in love with words that she assumed her teacher was wrong. More importantly, she kept on writing.

When Spinelli was nine years old, she discovered a new outlet for her desire: a red diary, with a key, which she was given

as a Christmas gift. Not knowing exactly what one was supposed to write in a diary, Spinelli chronicled the spectacular suc-
cesses of her childhood and adolescence—winning spelling bees
and poetry contests, collecting Girl Scout awards and school
medals. Along the way, she let go of her preoccupation with
life's large events. She has come to savor and value the tiny
spaces in between the honors and prizes. In her journals,
Spinelli now relishes life's small moments.

Spinelli watches each day unfold, honors being, not just
doing, and never discounts daily events as potential material for
her journal, or as a source for poems or picture books. Her collection of bedtime poems *Where Is the Night Train Going?* mirrors her delight in winding down the day with nighttime rituals:
reading, writing letters, and giving thanks for daily blessings.

At the end of each day, Spinelli climbs into bed with a cup of
tea to write in her journal. "I don't try to be literary," she says.
"I just let the words flow. My journals keep me centered, give
me a place to look back on and learn from."

In a journal entry dated November 24, 1997, Spinelli wrote
about the day's activities while on vacation at the beach:
"Walked . . . gathered shells in a zip-lock bag for the grandkids
. . . Scrabble games . . . reading and napping." On November
25, she recorded more mundane domestic duties: "Jerry and I
went to the Kimberton Farm Store for groceries. Did laundry . . . Caught
up on mail . . . ironed . . . roasted chestnuts . . . made blueberry
muffins." On December 10, 1997, it was raining, and Eileen had
a cold. She was taking her grape-flavored cough syrup, and husband Jerry was bringing her cups of lemon tea and saucers of
saltines. She napped and dreamed about lining up old chairs and
sofas along the curb.

To read her journal, she says, is to peek through a window to
her heart. It is also the window from which she views the world,
tracks her life and gains perspective on where she's been and
where she's going, personally and professionally. Her audience
is her six children, eleven grandchildren, and future great-

grandchildren, just in case they ever wonder what kind of woman she was. Their antics and sayings inhabit the pages of her journal and often find their way into her poetry and picture books. For example, her son once told her, "When you grow up you can be anything you want, but not an alligator." His words, which sat in her journal for many years, recently inspired her to write a picture book manuscript.

Following daily nine to noon shifts at her writing desk, Spinelli might take a few moments to write a sentence or two about the day's progress in a new endeavor—a professional journal. By reading back over this volume, she concludes that bad things pass, difficult manuscripts either get completed or tossed, and the world keeps going. She notices how peace replaces panic as work continues.

An avid reader of journals, Spinelli will buy any book in journal format. She learned from May Sarton, Dorothy Wordsworth, and Anne Truitt the value of journal writing to clarify one's ideas and feelings and to capture the details of life. She urges aspiring poets and journal keepers to inspect the little things, what one eats and the color of a favorite shirt. In her attention to daily detail, Spinelli honors the poet Milton who wrote in *Paradise Lost*, "That which before us lies in daily life/Is the prime wisdom."

Eileen Spinelli's books include

Somebody Loves You, Mr. Hatch
Where Is the Night Train Going?
If You Want to Find Golden
Lizzie Logan Wears Purple Sunglasses
Naptime/Laptime
When Mama Comes Home Tonight

The Interview

For Christmas when I was nine or ten I was given one of those red diaries with a key. Because of this gift, I started journal writing. Ever since I was a little girl I wanted to be a writer. I don't know what ever happened to those childhood diaries. The earliest ones in my possession come from my twenties.

Nowadays, keeping a journal is part of my nighttime ritual. I climb into bed with a cup of tea and my journal. How long I write depends on how tired I am and what I have to write about, but I do write every night. I try to capture as faithfully as possible my experience of that day. Ultimately, journal keeping is a way of tracking who I am, where I'm going, and where I've been.

Life's Daily Routines

As a child and even as a young adult I thought the important things in life were the spectacular things—winning a prize at school or other big events. Over the years I have come to savor and value the small events even more. I've come to believe that the small familiar things about our lives—the weather, what I had for lunch, dancing in the yard with a grandchild—are more important than they might seem.

Journal Companions

I'm fascinated by people's journals. When May Sarton died I felt sad for many reasons, but particularly sad because there wouldn't be any more of her journals. I admire her honesty.

I love the drawings in Jennifer Dewey's journals. I wish I could walk out my back door and sketch a tree or a spider. I have to overcome the idea that I'm not an artist and that it's OK if my leaf doesn't look like a leaf. Nobody is going to see my sketches anyway, but I have this block about drawing.

I've read the words of Emily Carr, whose journals [*Hundreds and Thousands: The Journals of Emily Carr*] are lyrical and very personal. I've read Dorothy Wordsworth's *Grasmere Journals* and Anne Truitt's *Daybook*. I'll buy any book in journal format.

Strictly Private

If you were to look in my journals you would be peeking through a window to my heart. It's also a window for me to look through and see who I am. I don't let anyone see my journals, but I do hope that one day my grandchildren and my great-grandchildren will be sitting around wondering what kind of a woman I was, thinking they would like to read my journals. I hope they do, so they will know me as a person.

I keep my journals in a box I call my life box. My daughter Molly decorated a wooden chest depicting different facets of my life. It's bigger than a bread box, but smaller than a hope chest.

Professional Journal

I thought it might be fun to track my writing life, so I've just begun keeping a record of current projects. It's helpful because I see how tentative I am at the beginning and how things I worry about then fall into place. The details are slim, just a couple of lines each day. It's helpful to me to go back and see that almost every time I start a project, I don't know where it's going or if it's going to work. Then it's nice to see that at least I finished it.

I reflect on my life as a writer in my main journal. If a publisher rejects a piece that I thought was good, I work it through in my journal. Tracking my work and my moods helps me see that bad things pass and difficult manuscripts either get finished or tossed and the world keeps going.

Cautions, Advice, and Guidelines

Journal writing slows me down and pushes me to take a look at my day, at myself, at what's happening around me. I encourage children to do likewise. Kids need a place to sort through their feelings, especially when they are going through a crisis.

From Eileen Spinelli's recent diary

The journal is a private place to bring up emotions and explore them. It's not only a place to keep in touch with who you are at the moment, it's a way of monitoring personal growth: so that's who I was in first grade and here I am now.

It's important for everybody, not just children, to honor being, not only doing. We get too caught up in doing, making, producing. The journal is a way to say this is who I am on the inside, and it's fine to be doing nothing but sitting here on the grass.

Although once in a while is better than never, I think it's good to make journal writing a daily habit. I'm too busy in the morning, so nighttime is best for me.

I believe it is important for children to express the whole fabric of their lives, not just the times they win the spelling bee. Record the smaller moments: what did I like to eat, what did my favorite shirt look like? By recording the smaller moments they learn the value of life as it unfolds each day.

Graham Salisbury

"Not Your Normal Beast"

Graham Salisbury as a teenager

He flunked English as a college freshman. Twice. He admits he didn't get a brain until age thirty. Until then, the closest he ever came to keeping a journal was collecting copies of songs from his days as a singer/songwriter. He wishes he had kept a journal when he was younger, especially during the great years of his life from seventh grade on. But Graham Salisbury was busy doing other things—wandering, drifting, surfing, skippering glass-bottom boats, working as deck hand on deep-sea fishing boats.

Music was his passion and, for a long time, his livelihood. Released as a single by CBS Records, and with Salisbury as a lead singer for the group Millenium, his song "Five A.M."

climbed to the top of the hit parade in the Phillipines. The Los Angeles music scene was too unpredictable and when he decided music wasn't going to be his life, Salisbury returned to college, this time wanting to be there. He earned straight A's and graduated with honors from California State University—Northridge.

During his days at Northridge, Salisbury developed an interest in young people. Volunteering as "Noon Goon" in nearby Tarzana Elementary School, he kept the peace on the playground so the teachers could eat lunch. After graduation, Salisbury earned a Montessori certificate in Italy and went on to teach elementary school.

He became a lover of books for young readers when he wandered into a bookstore and found Scott O'Dell's *Island of the Blue Dolphins*. He liked the cover, bought the book, and was dumbfounded by the quality of literature available for children. Loving reading, loving kids, it all seemed to fit together. When he discovered he could construct a decent sentence, he was on his way to writing for children. It would take him five years to teach himself how to write a publishable story. The result was his first novel, *Blue Skin of the Sea*. "I got lucky. It got published. Bingo. I was on a roll. I still am."

Salisbury feared his recently acquired brain wasn't all that trustworthy, so he turned to journal writing. The journal he slips into a back pocket is his private hiding place where he records experiences that tug at his heart or choke in his throat.

In the downtown Portland, Oregon, office where he writes—which he designed and decorated to fit his personality—he hides a shelf of journals behind closed cabinetry. A confessed visual organizer, Salisbury has arranged the journals by size, largest to smallest. When he needs to recharge his emotions, he opens a journal at random and takes a peek. Rereading, he remembers and is led into the deeper, emotional part of his writing.

"To live is to feel," he wrote in the essay "The Art of Beginnings," and "to feel is to live." By recording emotionally powerful moments, Salisbury fills his journals with things that have moved him. "It's like a safe deposit box for the important things in my life."

Salisbury prefers a journal he can fit into his back pocket, one with blank paper that feels smooth and cool to the touch. Exciting ideas pop up at weird times; he finds a portable journal works best. He likes to hatch his observations and ruminations, then let them fester and mature.

Salisbury, who suffers with advanced stages of the book-buying disease, wonders if a chapter of Journal Buyers Anonymous exists. He doesn't really want a cure, just somebody to understand his impulse to buy new journals, fill them partway, then search for another. If he could locate a leather-bound journal to carry in his back pocket, his life would be perfect. Then again, he kind of hopes he doesn't. It's always fun to keep looking.

Graham Salisbury's books include:

Under the Blood-Red Sun
Blue Skin of the Sea
Shark Bait
Jungle Dogs

The Interview

I first got the idea of keeping a journal because I wanted to save some of the funny things my kids did. My son Keenan once asked: "Does God have armpits?" Hah! How could I ever let that go? It was beautiful. So innocently asked. I never kept a journal as a kid because I didn't get a brain until I was over thirty. After I got a brain I became a reader and I wanted to keep track of what I read, and I wanted to copy down fine examples of writing to keep and read and be inspired by. I still do this. I wish now as a writer that I had kept a book of thoughts and events from childhood. That would be so informative. As it is, I have to depend on memory, which fortunately is still intact.

Gifts from the Universe

Now I use journals not so much as a source of ideas, but more a key to memories. They hold a gold mine of ideas and feelings and passing thoughts. And memories are key for a writer. How could I possibly write about love without remembering how love felt—painful! And wonderful. And certainly incomprehensible.

Memories are gifts from the universe. For example, just opening my journal at random I see that in 1992 I wrote this: "Age 17 — Flying to Honolulu out of Kamuela in a single-engine plane and experiencing weightlessness out over Alenuihaha channel, too young to fear." That entry jars me back to those days of fearlessness, or stupidity, as I think of it now. I may use that memory sometime, somehow. I can still feel the thrilling, tingling freefall as the pilot, one of my high school teachers, grinned as he shut the engine down and let the plane fall toward the ocean. My God, how did I live past my teenage years?

A Clean Page and Mechanical Pencil

At first I used the kind with lines, but for the past several years I've used only the clean-page kind. I won't use lined journals again because they are too neat. A journal should be a place to wander, to draw, to scribble, to explore. A clean page is freedom. As for size, I like them big enough to do some damage in, and small enough to carry. Quality paperback book size is my preference. I also like cool paper, hand-made or recycled. Eye-burning white is nice, crisp.

I tried using my computer as a journal but did not like it. I love to write on my computer, but for a journal it doesn't work for me. Too sterile. I love mechanical pencils, fine-point, the sleek, expensive kind.

Fickle Attraction

I've been trying to be an honest journal-keeper for years and years and years. I have twenty or more journals that are partially written in. I have come to the conclusion that I am not bad or stupid or lazy, I am simply a busy person, and keeping a journal is time consuming and my inspiration to write in them is sporadic. We've separated a time or two, gone out and had affairs with toys and other distractions, but have managed to get back together for spells at a time. We are both quite fickle. My journal is too demanding and straight-laced, and I am too lazy and loose, but we love each other nevertheless. Most of the time I'd rather be writing books or playing my guitar or wrestling with my boys or having a lemonade in the sun with my wife, Robyn.

Tips for Journal Keepers

The first thing you need to do is get a journal. Use whatever feels good in your hands. This is important. You want to love it so much that you keep it with you. Find a pen or pencil that fits you, that feels good in your hand, that writes nice, that smells good or looks good or tastes good when you chew on it. You have to like your tools. Then write in the journal, some little or big thing every day, and not stuff like "Today I went over to Jacky's house and ..." No. That will be useless to you. Rather, write stuff like, "Dad kissed me on the head today just before he left for work. He never kisses me like that, and I wonder what's going on." Stuff like that—feelings, emotions. Good, meaty stuff. No one else will ever read your journal if you take care first to tell everyone in your family to keep their grubby mitts off your STUFF, and then hide it somewhere. Your journal is your private place to say stuff, to spout off, to laugh and cry and complain. All you have to do is get started and make a habit of keeping it up. Fairly soon you will not be able to live without it. And that's a nice place to reach.

6/90

Yesterday I was in a huge hurry to get home, driving in slow traffic down by Portland Civic Auditorium. A man was driving in front of me with his wife in the front seat and two teenage sons in the back. Stop, go, stop, go... slow, slow, slow! Finally, he stopped in the right-hand turn lane at the corner of a block to let one of his sons out, blocking me and forcing me to wait.

I became frustrated but managed, thank God, to keep from honking at them. The mother got out and held her seat back for one of the boys to get out. Apparently he was headed for something going on at the Civic. He was young, maybe 14, and off in the big city on his own. To say goodbye to him, his mother put her hand on his cheek and looked into his eyes with the most beautiful, loving look on her face. The moment was so tender it broke my heart down to where it should have been all along. Instantly, all my frustration left me. There is great and wonderful power in such a simple act of love, even to those of us who only manage to observe.

Graham Salisbury illustrates his diary

James Cross Giblin

"Working with Words"

James Cross Giblin in Central
Park, 1956

For his tenth birthday James Cross Giblin received his first journal and started writing about one of his great and enduring loves—the movies. Thereafter, his diary contained a record of favorite screen stars and films, his predictions for the Academy Awards, a list of movies viewed and plays attended.

> December 31, 1946: For the best movie of 1946, I believe my award will go to two pictures, both dramas: *Rebecca* (a revival) and *The Seventh Veil*.
> The best female performance was given by Olivia deHavilland in *To Each His Own*.
> The best male performance was given by Claude Rains in

Deception and *Caesar and Cleopatra.*

The best psycological (sic) mystery was *Undercurrent*; with its star, Katharine Hepburn, it was great.

The best western was *San Antonio* with Errol Flynn.

The best cartoon was Walt Disney's *Bath Day.*

The poorest picture of 1946 was *Masquerade in Mexico* with Dorothy Lamour.

For a shy child who was dunked in a nursery school swim class then later teased and chased by the second-grade bully, the real world was a difficult place to navigate. Part of that boy might have enjoyed the company of children; another part was inclined to hang back, afraid of the unfamiliar, potentially harmful world his father Edward Kelley Giblin had cautioned him about. Adolescence only intensified a natural inclination to look within.

Had it not been for his ninth-grade English teacher who suggested he help with the class newspaper, Giblin might have plunged deep into isolation. Caught up in the writing and editing of a modest, mimeographed publication, Giblin discovered a love for words and the joy of working with classmates.

In the fall of 1955, after completing college and graduate school, Giblin moved to New York City and began regularly to keep a personal journal. Using ruled college notebooks he captured surrounding scenes—the daily and mundane against a backdrop of cityscapes and skyscrapers. Making hand-written entries, Giblin stilled the rush of external sensations and experiences. Journal keeping became his means of recognizing themes and patterns in his life and balancing competing pulls of inner and outer worlds during confusing transitions.

December 27, 1955: Central Park was beautiful this afternoon, with a brisk wind blowing and all the lakes, pools, and streams heavily iced. Little boys were everywhere, alone, in pairs, and in packs, ranging over every rock, slope, and high crevasse, scaring the squirrels, who took to the trees.

I saw one pair of little boys, the older not more than six, the younger probably four, who had climbed high up a sheer rock slope overlooking the lake. The smaller one slipped as I watched from a path across a rocky gulf, and almost slid off the black, smooth rock. But he grabbed the older one's foot (the older one promptly grabbed onto a handy young tree trunk) and hung on, desperately, whimpering a little, his eyes closed tight to the frozen lake far below him. The older one, still keeping one hand firmly on the tree trunk, reached down with the other and slowly, gently pulled the younger boy onto the safe, top flatness of the rock.

When he reached safety, the little one stopped whimpering, and after only a brief moment, began to jump about, and laugh, and shout, as if nothing had ever, or could ever possibly happen to him. I moved on.

April 21, 1956: Today I saw Uta Hagen in Turgenev's *A Month in the Country* at the Phoenix Theatre, and had time to explore the Second Avenue neighborhood before the show. A conglomeration of Jewish delicatessens, shops, and restaurants, with a great number of makeshift theatres on second floors and in basements, all proclaimed by arty, often hand-printed, posters.

The beautiful old stone "Church of the Bouwerie" dominates one corner near St. Mark's Place, and a group of women and young men were working in the sun in the churchyard, behind its high grill fence, planting tulip bulbs, probably in preparation for the church's tulip festival, announced on the bulletin board for May 12.

There was a joy and beauty in their faces as they worked, almost as if they were planting a part of themselves with the bulbs. Several people stopped outside the fence to watch them work. That's all. Just to watch. And something close to envy touched their faces as they watched, as if they wished one of those working would invite them to come behind the fence and help with the planting.

As his career developed and flourished during the next forty years, Giblin wrote faithfully in his journal. There, as in his work, he honed his skills as author and editor, polishing each entry as if he were preparing his private reflections for public consumption. Abruptly, however, in 1991, Giblin closed his personal journal and abandoned the chronicle that until then had mediated his internal and external realities. Now stored in his New York apartment, Giblin's spiral notebooks, each about a hundred pages, span the entire top shelf of his office closet. He rarely consults them, feeling less of a need to revisit past feelings and occurrences.

Uncertain why he set aside his personal journal, Giblin suspects a fall from a dais and the resulting severe injury were a turning point in his life. Recuperating at home set him musing on mortality, the narrowing of time, and the need to focus his energies on the present and the future. Nevertheless, he continued to reflect about writing and career struggles in the professional journal he began in the late 1970s.

In a 1993 excerpt from this Writing Workbook, Giblin confesses to feelings of inadequacy and periods of procrastination. What was to become his highly acclaimed book *When Plague Strikes* was taking much longer than anticipated. After venting fears and frustrations, Giblin reminds himself to give the subject all the time and attention it deserves. Promising not to make unreasonable demands on himself, he soothes self-doubt and returns to the manuscript.

January 25, 1993—Monday morning: Yesterday I discussed the content and focus of the Plague book in a long phone conversation with Sue [Sue Alexander, a writer friend], and came up with some good ideas that I want to record here before I forget any of them.

1. The book should be aimed at ten-year-olds and up, not young adults.

2. It should not be a history of epidemic disease, as *Walls* evolved into a history of fortification and *Let There Be Light* into a history of windows, but should rather be limited to dramatic accounts of no more than four diseases that (a) had a disastrous initial impact on the affected populations, and (b) left lasting social, political,

religious, and cultural consequences in their wake.

3. The diseases to be included—subject to change in the light of further research—will probably be the Black Death, smallpox (which decimated the native populations of the Americas), influenza, and AIDS. Many other diseases could be covered, of course: tuberculosis, cholera, malaria, infantile paralysis, etc. But I feel those I've chosen had a more startling and terrible impact than the others. I may be wrong about cholera, and perhaps it should be dealt with also; we'll see.

4. Besides the in-depth central chapters, there should also be an introductory chapter to set the scene—perhaps with an ancient Greek or Roman plague—and define the scope of the book. Then, at the end, there should be a concluding chapter which will make the point that the battle against epidemic disease is an ongoing one to which the best efforts of all peoples must be devoted. In other words, it's not simply an American concern, but one that extends worldwide.

Additional problems with focus may arise in the course of the research and writing, but for the first time I feel as if I have a workable grip on this project. Thank you, Sue—and also the members of Barbara Seuling's writing class, on whom I tried out some of these ideas last Wednesday evening.

Giblin credits his relaxed, conversational writing tone in part to his years as a journal keeper. Whenever someone asks how to get started as a writer, he always recommends keeping a journal. "Be as honest as you can and write to please only yourself. Keep it under lock and key, if necessary." Out of his love for language he worked, even in the privacy of his own journal, to form flawless sentences and sculpt his craft. Entries from his journals highlight Giblin's sensitivity to the world around him, his gift of observation, and his artistry in translating city graphics into clear, compelling prose.

In his award-winning nonfiction books for juvenile readers, Giblin distills complex concepts and breathes life into distant dates and facts. Offering readers immediate, human connections to historic moments from long ago, Giblin invites them to step onto the stage of history. The distinctive voice James Cross Giblin brings to children's literature has evolved from the other great and enduring love of his life—working with words.

James Cross Giblin's books include

Charles A. Lindbergh: A Human Hero
When Plague Strikes: The Black Death, Smallpox, AIDS
Thomas Jefferson: A Picture Book Biography
The Truth About Unicorns
The Riddle of the Rosetta Stone: Key to Ancient Egypt
Writing Books for Young People (for adults)

The Interview

I kept a journal for a very brief period when I was about ten. Somebody gave me a diary as a present, and I made a list of the movies I saw for about six months. I was movie crazy at that age. Occasionally I added a brief comment, but it was mainly the title of the movie and who was in it and the theater where I saw it in my hometown of Painesville, Ohio, a suburb of Cleveland. I came across that diary when I was closing up my family home after my mother's death a few years back and I kept it, of course, brought it here to New York. It's kind of fun, but suddenly it breaks off and I have no idea why I stopped keeping it.

I began a real journal in the late fall of 1955, which was my first year on my own here in New York. I was just out of college and trying to figure out what I wanted to do, what I could do, and how to make a living in the meantime. I remember being assaulted by so many different sensations and experiences that fall, from the most mundane, like the need to buy towels, to much, much more weighty and personal issues of different kinds. I think I was afraid of drowning in confusion in New York unless I kept some record of my life at that time. I guess I was looking for themes and patterns in it, I'm not sure. But I know the journal helped a great deal. It was quite therapeutic, although it was mainly a way to keep things straight.

I wrote in the journal pretty regularly until after an accident in the fall of 1991.

Letting Go

I can describe this change in my journal keeping practices, but I haven't figured out why it occurred. The accident happened at a sales conference just after I'd mounted the steps to a dais. I thought the dais went to the back of the meeting room but it didn't. So instead of crossing the floor to take my seat at the table, I stepped off into space. I fell about two and a half feet and somehow managed to end up on my back.

I was fortunate to have come out of that with only a badly sprained ankle. I didn't break anything. Later I decided I had blacked out the moment I realized I was in mid-air and must have gone limp. That's probably what saved me. Anyway, in the wake of the accident I had to use a cane for a few weeks. The swelling took a long time to go down, and I had to wear one of those medical shoes, with straps and velcro, on my left foot. I didn't want to dwell on my condition in my journal. I'd done all the research for my next book and I wanted to work on something objective, something beyond myself.

So I concentrated on the book and let the journal go. And I never really took it up again. There have been a few scattered entries since December 1991, but the last volume of the journal is still the one I was writing in just before that accident. At the time I interpreted this as just not wanting to dwell on every twitch of my poor injured ankle. I also think I had an urge to go ahead with my life, even though I couldn't walk easily. I wanted to put my energy into writing for an audience instead of just for me. I wanted to keep moving forward. The main thing the accident did for me was to make me aware of mortality in a different way, and of time and age. What came into focus for me was that writing for others seemed a more valuable pursuit than contemplating my own navel.

The Professional Diary

Once I started writing books regularly, which was in the late '70s, early '80s, I began to keep a concurrent writing workbook, which has taken the place of the old journal in many ways. I also keep lists of things I need to do, professional things. I do a monthly list of the writing tasks, the editing tasks, the lecturing tasks that lie ahead, and I also keep a record of fees I'm expecting. In between all this practical stuff I will often, if I'm feeling troubled about the way a book is going or if I get an idea for something new and I'm fooling around with it, exploring whether I really want to pursue it—I'll put all that into the writing workbook. It has become a professional journal.

Audience, Honesty, and Privacy

My audience for the journal has always been myself; I've never shared the journal with anyone. I'm single and consequently have no children around, so there's less chance of somebody else reading the journal. I've never practiced self-censorship. As a matter of fact, some of my entries from earlier years would probably seem quite graphic to a stranger.

You can't write a journal if you're thinking of an audience first rather than yourself. A journal at its best should be a completely free and open conversation with yourself. You really have to trust and open yourself up if you're going to keep a journal. If you don't there's not much point in it. Ideally one should probably keep two journals—one for public consumption and another strictly private, where nothing needs to be left out.

Personal Journals and Historical Research

In recording events and people in a journal it is hard to capture the full picture. You always have to keep that fact in mind when consulting diaries and journals for research purposes. The journal will reflect one point of view, the way the writer saw the events as he or she lived through them. It may not be the whole picture.

If possible, the researcher should try to find other accounts of the same event. I could imagine, for example, that a first-person account of the German air raids on London during WWII would give readers a vivid picture of living through air raids. For a wider view of the Blitz one should consult more general histories of that period in the war.

Whether you're writing for an audience or just for yourself, there is always a tendency to make yourself look better in a situation than you may have actually performed because you're seeing it from your point of view. No matter how hard one strives for honesty or to tell the whole truth about a situation or relationship, it's bound to be colored by one's own perceptions and sense of self.

Recently I have been reading all of the volumes of Anne Morrow Lindbergh's journals, diaries, and letters as research for a biography I'm writing of Charles Lindbergh. Inevitably I compare how she approached events and recorded them with memories of my own journal writing, and I find myself wondering what she left out.

For instance, she has entries about her response to the kidnapping of her firstborn son and to the trial of Bruno Hauptmann for the crime two years later. But I keep having the feeling that she either may not have written about her deeper feelings at those times or she chose to expunge them from the record when she prepared her journals for publication.

There are many entries about so-and-so coming to lunch and that she had a vivacious personality, that kind of thing, which gives a picture of Lindbergh's circle of friends and her life, certainly. There's not a single criticism of Charles, though, and I don't believe her. I'm not saying they had a bad marriage; I don't think they did, but everybody gets annoyed and tired and flares up at friends and companions sometimes. That's part of life, but it's not reflected here. Over and over it's "C,"—she always calls him "C,"—"C is so strong, so right." I almost feel like saying, "Come off it."

Then there's the issue of self censorship. When the writer is writing for public consumption there is the tendency to protect, to leave out certain personal material. Before my mother died, I tried to get her to write a brief autobiography. I said it was only for me and that I would very much like to have it. She started it but wrote just to the point when she met my father. She stopped it there. She said she just didn't want to go on beyond that point. I found that very interesting.

My parents had a very solid marriage. They were both strong-willed, independent people with strong personalities. My mother was a very honest person who was perfectly willing to confront personal issues. But she was also of a certain generation and she didn't want to share those things with anyone, even me.

Journal as Haven

The journal is my refuge where I can be completely myself. It's a very cozy, safe, comfortable space. Actually it's like the home office I have now. It's a corner room with windows on two sides and views of New York skyscrapers, but it's close enough to the street so that I don't feel disconnected. It's a haven. I think we all need havens.

Writing, not necessarily journal writing, is another haven for me. I feel frustrated if I don't have at least a couple hours a day by myself at my desk. Even though I may have accomplished a lot that day in terms of phone calls or getting necessary chores done—a dentist's appointment or whatever—I feel as though I've wasted the day if I don't write at least a few paragraphs.

Judith Logan Lehne

"Taking off My Masks"

Judith Logan Lehne in fourth grade

From the time she first held a pencil, author Judith Logan Lehne has put her thoughts and feelings down on paper. The result: more than seventy published stories and articles, two nonfiction books, two children's novels, and stacks of plastic milk crates filled with journals.

At age twelve, Lehne received her first diary and started writing to an imaginary friend, Sue. Having no idea what she was supposed to write, she watched her older sister for clues. It must have been something important, she concluded, because her sister wrote late into the night, then locked her diary and hid it away.

In time, what Lehne tapped through diary writing was a deep

vein of emotions she grew up believing girls weren't supposed to have. Her early diaries are filled with expressions of happiness, confusion, and hardship as well as observations about her family's emotional life. On July 15, 1960, she notes, "Last full day at the cottage. Something very funny happened: Bob and Dave capsized the canoe. Back on the dock, they laughed for three minutes without stopping." On December 11, 1960, she confides to Sue: "I want to get away from Mom and Dad and the kids for a long time. All they ever do is disagree with and scream at me. Why?"

"I leapt through life," she has written, "embracing all the joy, laughter, struggle, and adventure it had to offer." As time permitted, she captured all this in her journal. Her list of New Year's resolutions during her freshman year in high school includes references to the roller coaster of emotions she rode, sometimes with carefree abandon, sometimes holding on tight: "1. no matter how hard, try to hold my temper" and "4. keep calm when around boys and don't act jeuvenile [sic]."

As a college freshman, when she was "too busy doing life to record it," she made notes on calendars. Love had found its way into her emotional repertoire: February 4, 1966: "Junior Prom wk-nd at Princeton . . . go to see Rick. love is a many splendored thing!"

"With every ounce of enthusiasm I can muster," Lehne says, "I encourage children to keep journals, not on a rigid schedule, but when there is a need to express feelings." For Lehne, emotions are the key to creating fictional characters readers care about—living, breathing, multidimensional characters children can put their arms around, not flat, cookie-cutter ones, no matter how well-decorated.

When Lehne visits classrooms as author-in-residence, she helps students explore their secret caves of emotions and use this knowledge to create three-dimensional, flesh-and-blood characters to populate their own stories. Through a series of interactive exercises, she leads students into their interiors to identify their feelings, then guides them in interpreting the outward signs of emotion others broadcast. Lehne believes that being able to put feelings into words is the most important skill a writer can develop. It is a talent she has been honing since her early days as a diary keeper when she confronted her personal monsters and identified the power of raw emotions. Through journal writing she uncovered her deeply rooted emotional life; through fiction, she gave it wings.

In her social world as writer, teacher, mother, and placement counselor for Job Corps students, Lehne wears many masks. When she reaches for her journal, she is able to put her multiple roles aside and explore any issue, however emotional. Throughout the years, her journals have come in many forms—envelopes filled with scraps of paper, photos with notations on the back, notebooks tied with ribbon, lined paper, blank paper, hardback, paperback, and calendars. She compares her journals to a quilt, tattered with rough spots, threadbare in places, but homemade. In the northwoods of Wisconsin where she lives and writes, they keep her warm and ignite her writing.

Judith Logan Lehne's books include

Never Be Bored Book: Things to Do When There's Nothing to Do
Kangaroos for Kids
When the Ragman Sings
Coyote Girl

The Interview

My older sister had secrets. Every night she would keep the light on late to write in her diary. When I got a diary for Christmas, I had no idea what I was supposed to write, but since my sister kept hers locked away, I figured I had to write something important. Here's a sample from my first diary: "Bobby looked at me. George looked at me."

My early diaries had little locks that any nosy brother or sister or parent could pick. I kept much of what I wrote as a child hidden—I'd take out the pages I didn't want my parents to see and shove them under my mattress.

Fantasy Trips

My diary was an imaginary friend or pen pal and I named her Sue. I found my emotions through writing in my diary. One day I sat down to write in Sue and spewed out anger and sadness. I had tapped emotions I thought girls weren't supposed to have.

In high school, I lied in my diaries. "Bobby Smith asked me out and I almost fainted." Bobby Smith hadn't asked me out, but I wrote a fantasy about what I wanted to happen. I worried about this lying until I decided to be a fiction writer.

Off with My Masks

Today my journal is a concrete representation of a me that I don't know in any other form. It goes beyond my public persona, beyond anything that I might speak out loud. Interacting in the world, in the social world, I wear many masks, but when I go to my journal, I'm stripped of my masks. While my journals let me see how far I've come, they also throw new challenges at me. I take great comfort in being able to identify my monsters, which often surface when I write in my journal. Journal writing also tempers my emotions and clarifies and dilutes the raw emotions. Journal writing lets me purge emotionally so that I can intellectually figure out what to do. In this way it becomes a valuable tool for moving me forward in my life.

I don't hide my journals away anymore. I don't like locking away the core of who I am. I uncovered my inner child through journal writing and I have given her wings; to put her in a drawer or under the mattress doesn't feel right to me. If people can't respect my privacy, they deserve to see what they are going to see, ready or not.

I have absolutely no journal writing routine. Usually I write at night because that's when I can best turn off all of my should's and have to's. I'm too tired to should and have to, so I just vent. I let my pen be a channel from my soul. My brain is disengaged. I don't think to myself, "Now what would my editor say?"

My journal is like a soft, tattered quilt; some rough spots, threadbare in places, but it's real, handmade and it keeps me warm. A friend is someone who knows all of your weaknesses, all of your flaws and ugly spots, and still loves you. My journal is like that quilt, like that friend.

Journals, Journals Everywhere

I keep several kinds of journals—envelopes filled with scraps of paper, photos with notes on the backs, notebooks. The journal that I have been using recently is a journal entitled "The Goddess Within." It's got wonderful line drawings of goddess figures along with quotes by women and information about the archaeological finds related to goddess worship in the past. When I'm writing in this journal I have a feeling of being connected with a spirit, a sense of a higher power. Though I'm not a goddess worshiper, at the time I started that journal I needed a feminine sense of God.

I have notebooks tied with ribbons, notebooks with blank pages, sometimes hardbound, more recently paperback. I don't feel I have to fill one up before I start another. If I want a journal for a different reason, I will find one to fit that purpose. If I include journals, calendars, every scrap of paper I've journaled on, every photograph I've saved, I'd need several plastic milk crates to hold them all.

Heart to Heart

Since I write for children, I want to connect to them emotionally. I want my characters to be people who feel. In my journals, I explore all my personal issues, especially ones that go back to childhood. Journal writing is a technique that shows up

New Year
Resolutions for
1962

1. No matter how hard, try to hold my temper.
2. Try to do better in school.
3. Keep my room clean
4. Keep calm when around boys and don't act jeuvenile.
5. Be a better friend to Martha, Candy, Linda, Pat and especially Leslie.
6. Be more helpful
7. Be more appreciative of things done for me.
8. Try to remember that mother and Dad used to be teenagers once, too.

From Judith Logan Lehne's childhood diary

in my fiction. Billie, the main character in *Coyote Girl*, keeps a sketchbook in which she plans and fantasizes about the future. That's the way I kept my journal in high school.

Writers need to know every emotion possible and know so concretely that they can get them on the page in a way young readers understand. This is not about technique. It has to do with tapping your own emotions and writing about them through your own experience.

Family Chronicle

My mother died when I was eighteen. She kept no records of the time of my birth, when I crawled, when I talked, what my first words were. Since I had not thought to ask about those things until after I had children of my own, I feel like a part of me—of my history—is missing.

After my kids were born I began logs of their childhoods—Tessa got her first tooth today, Todd had stitches removed at 4:00—bits and pieces of day-to-day living. I want my children to be able to look back and see what happened in our lives as a family, remember things that they didn't take the time to journal about because they were too busy living life. What drove me to do this kind of calendar journal-keeping was the hole in my own life. I've always had a fear that I would die and leave my children with the same kind of voids that I had.

Of course my children will inherit all of my journals. Then they will know my deepest, darkest secrets. But I don't mind because I believe it will give them permission to experience any emotions that pull at them and it will guide them about ways to purge through writing about their more problematic emotions.

Celebration Time

With every ounce of enthusiasm I have, I encourage children to keep journals. No matter what, keep a journal. Not every day or on a schedule, but whenever there is a need to express feelings. Children need to know that no one is going to invade their privacy, and parents must respect that privacy.

If we want to raise children to be compassionate adults, skilled at self-analysis, we should encourage teachers to set aside classroom time for journal writing. Even if students just free-write about a class and their feelings about a class, they are making discoveries. I don't think that the teacher should grade (or even read) this kind of personal writing. Journal writing should be a time of self-examination, fun, and celebration.

Journal Disaster

Whenever I went to my children's activities and sporting events, I always kept a journal in my purse to record observations: something overheard, an accent or snippet of dialogue, a person or scene I wanted to describe. Perhaps it was a smell that came through the air, whatever. Or I'd ramble about how I felt at the time: "I think my butt is going to rot on these wooden bleachers . . . I'm so sick of sitting here." Or I might be describing someone everyone knew: "Joy's hair looks like a wreck today."

The last time I used this notebook I was sitting in the bleachers waiting for the band to strike up. I described some of the people in the audience and recorded what the teenagers sitting around me were saying. I don't know what ever happened to that journal, whether it fell through the bleachers when I stood up or if I mislaid it. I never found it. It's out there. Fortunately my name was not on it, but in a small town, when you refer to your children by their first names, well, anyone can put it together. All I can hope is that some kid found it, opened it up, decided it was worthless, and threw it in the garbage.

Jacqueline Woodson

"Going to My Room and Closing the Door"

Jacqueline Woodson

Somewhere back in the fourth or fifth grade, Jacqueline Woodson awoke to the realization that America didn't welcome her or the people she loved. Poverty, crime, and drugs ravaged her neighborhood. On the national scene, Watergate and Vietnam—corruption and war—dominated the headlines. President Nixon had just resigned in disgrace. Woodson assumed George McGovern would take his place. After all, everyone in her neighborhood liked McGovern because he cared for black people. But when Gerald Ford took the oath of office,

Woodson remembers becoming sullen, then argumentative with her teachers and disconnected from her classmates. She hid under the porch and spent hours writing poetry in a journal.

"I stepped outside of the world," she wrote in the essay "A Sign of Having Been Here." "From this vantage point, I watched and took note."

Inside her journal, Woodson found freedom. She discovered a place to be alone and completely herself. Today she still retreats to her journal when she is upset. "When I open my journal, it feels like I'm a child going into my room and closing the door. Exaltation. Exhale. Freedom inside my space."

Woodson, who doesn't flinch from presenting truths about modern American life, admits that writing a novel is easier than committing personal truths to the pages of her journal because in fiction she can hide behind the characters she creates. If she hesitates to speak her deepest truths, it is because of a nagging thought: "Maybe I shouldn't write this. Maybe someone will find it." When she was a child, that someone was her younger brother. He not only read her journal, he blabbed Woodson's secrets to their grandmother. Woodson says she struggles to give herself permission to tell the truth and not let this fear of self expression stunt her growth as a woman or as a writer.

Woodson doesn't consult her journals as a source for writing fiction, but she has come to know that her characters' struggles often echo her own. In the 1980s, for example, she moved from Brooklyn to California, leaving her friends, family, and writing community behind. At the time, she was writing *Maizon at Blue Hill,* a story about a girl at boarding school who aches for old friends and family. Until Woodson went back and read journals from this period in her life, she hadn't recognized the connecting links between the emotional dimensions of her own life and the challenges facing her fictional protagonist.

Journal writing, she finds, supports her fiction in two ways: it frees her emotionally so she can explore her characters more fully and it brings her to her human foundation. From this place,

Woodson writes about issues facing preteens and teens.

Usually late in the evening, or when she's very upset, Woodson opens her leather-bound, 11-by-14-inch journal to calm her racing thoughts and thumping pulse. Relaxing is not an easy task for this prolific author who constantly thinks she should be working on a novel. Sometimes, just to still herself, she'll sit in the living room and sketch the fireplace. Lately, she's been typing entries at the computer then taping them into her journal. The result is a relaxed flow of words, more stream-of-consciousness than her deliberate hand-written entries. Journal writing is Woodson's way of communicating with herself. It is so essential to her life that whatever the demands of her writing schedule, she makes time for her journal.

Woodson remembers her days in elementary school when writing was a form of punishment: "an essay about why I misbehaved or ten thousand times on the board 'I will not . . .'" As a visiting author in the schools she delights in the emphasis on creative writing. By telling their stories, creating books and poems, children validate their lives. Write every day, Woodson urges them. Write for a half hour, maybe two. Write letters to friends, create short stories, or write in a journal.

Jacqueline Woodson's books include

The Dear One
Maizon at Blue Hill
I Hadn't Meant to Tell You This
From the Notebooks of Melanin Sun
The House You Pass on the Way
If You Come Softly

The Interview

I've always kept a journal since the fourth or fifth grade, though back then it was called a diary. My big sister had one and, of course, I wanted everything my big sister had. I wrote about school happenings and the trauma of the moment. I had all these—quote, unquote—boyfriends, and we weren't allowed to have boyfriends. My little brother Roman would find my journals and tell my grandmother about the boys I liked and kissed. Of course, he didn't reveal his source, so my grandmother assumed I had been talking to my friends.

My grandmother took me aside and reminded me that I wasn't to be dating. And she said, "You know you really shouldn't tell your friends everything because they'll sometimes come back and tell other people." I remember how frustrating it was because I couldn't tell the truth. I couldn't say, no, I didn't tell my friends and they told Roman. I couldn't say Roman took my journal out of the drawer and read it and tattled on me because then I'd be telling on myself. I just told her no, that didn't happen.

This experience impacted on how I keep journals now. Sometimes when I'm writing I think, maybe I shouldn't write this because someone will find it. And it stunts me. That's been my struggle—to write through that. When I die I don't care who reads what, but as a living person, I think, yeah, there's a lot in here that I don't want a whole lot of people to have access to.

The Whole Truth

Journal writing happens whenever I have the time, and that is usually late in the evening or whenever I'm really upset. When I'm frustrated it's hard for me to sit down and concentrate on writing fiction. Journaling helps me write through my trauma of the moment so that I can get back to the place where I can write creatively. When I open my journal it feels like I'm a child going into my room and closing the door. Exaltation. Exhale. Freedom inside my space. It's a place where I can tell the truth, 100 percent, and be who I am.

Writing All the Time

I think about writing all the time, and when I'm journaling I think maybe I should be working on a novel, or maybe I should be working on a picture book. Sketching in my journal allows me to relax my mind a bit. I use black art books, leather-bound, 11-by-14. I like the space and blank pages and the way I have a palette in front of me.

I just started a new format of journaling on my computer, which I try to do three or four times a week. I print out those entries and tape them into my journal. The writing flows much more easily because I type much faster than by hand. Writing by hand is more contemplative and slower. I write my novels longhand. When I'm writing on the computer, it's more stream of consciousness.

Journal Writing vs. Novel Writing

My journal writing is separate from my novel writing because it's about things I would never put in novel form. I don't go back to my journals as a source for writing fiction, but if you were to go back and read my journal, you could figure out why I was writing the novel I was writing at that time. Back in the 1980s I moved to California and left my whole community behind. I missed my friends back home, my family, and I was struggling to find a writers' community. At the time I was writing *Maizon at Blue Hill*, which is about a girl who misses her friends and family. I didn't know until I went back and read my journal how my life paralleled my character's struggle. Then I could say, oh, this is where that episode for the story came from. Not so much the character and voice—that's another struggle.

In my journal it's more about my day to day life and what the crises in that life are. Creative writing has always been an escape, and it's easier to do. In order to have a chronicle of my own life, and something to look back on, journal writing stays important. It is a way of communicating to myself. Whatever my writing schedule, I keep time for my journal.

Creating Characters

Journal writing frees me up to explore my fictional characters. It brings me to a human foundation so I can see the characters as fully human, especially when I have to write evil characters. There are more sides to them and that's about knowing and understanding my own everyday actions when I don't behave in the best manner.

Novel writing is an easier place to go to because I can hide behind the characters I create. These characters aren't me, they're something I've created.

I usually give my characters something that is important to me, like journaling. In *The Notebooks of Melanin Sun* I was trying to create this boy and I knew nothing about trying to figure out who he was. One of the characteristics I gave him was his notebooks. The postcards in *I Hadn't Meant to Tell You This* come from the poetry in my journal. There are also little observances, ticket stubs from a Monkees concert, and photographs. I'm generally a bad saver. I'm a stickler for space and organization and I don't like a lot of paper around. But I save letters and postcards. If something is evocative and might inspire me later, I'll save it.

Jean Craighead George

"In the Journal Lies the Story"

Jean Craighead George, age 12,
with pet screech owl

When she began keeping a diary at age ten, Jean Craighead George already knew she wanted to be a writer. Born into a family of naturalists, her childhood centered around nature and writing. Always drawn to the outdoors, she fished, caught frogs, and rode hay wagons with her brothers. On weekend hikes, her entomologist father taught her to identify plants and animals and how to make a meal from the land. Their home bustled with owls, falcons, raccoons, crickets, turtles, and dogs.

Her older twin brothers, now experts on Yellowstone's grizzly bears, dominated her, the household, and the neighborhood. They organized all the activities—from climbing down rainspouts to spelunking. One day, she remembers, she made the drastic mistake of reading them a poem from her diary. "Oh, that's terrible," they said. When she threatened to throw her diary out the window, they told her to go ahead. To her dismay, she did. What she learned from that experience, she says, was to become her own critic and keep things to herself.

During college, George shifted from the daily recounting of events, which she calls diary keeping, to sketchier, more impressionistic note taking, or journal keeping. As a newspaper reporter for the International News Service and the *Washington Post*, and later as a feature writer for United Press International, George began writing material necessary to her work in spiral tablets. But since 1948, when she published *Vulpes the Red Fox*, George has kept separate secretarial tablets for each children's book undertaken.

She says that her journal is a "jerky combination of observations, sketches, notes, and quotes." Five and a half feet of her diaries and journals line a shelf in her home in Chappaqua, New York, and serve as reference books for her professional writing. When she wrote *There's An Owl in the Shower*, for example, she turned to her childhood diaries to recall how she and her brothers had kept owls as kids. Young owls cuddled under their chins and sat on their shoulders.

When George is in the field researching a story, she writes or sketches in her journal as part of her daily routine. As she takes research notes, records personal observations, and draws, her story line evolves.

Before writing her Newbery Medal winner *Julie of The Wolves*, George spent the summer of 1970 studying wolves at the Naval Arctic Research Laboratory in Barrow, Alaska. On assignment for *Reader's Digest*, where she was a staff writer, George worked with Dr. J. Edgar Folk, a physiologist, and Dr. Michael Fox, a psychologist and veterinarian. Fox taught her the ways in which wolves communicate: eye contact, vocalization—including whimpering and howling, and body language.

In her autobiography, *Journey Inward*, George recounts the story of her repeated efforts to communicate with Silver, a mother wolf at the laboratory. Finally, one afternoon, in response to George's soft whimpering, Silver pulled back her lips and made eye contact. She wagged her tail, whimpered back, and tugged at George's coat sleeve. George understood Silver's message but didn't know how to tell her that she couldn't come live with her, even though she wanted to.

Later that summer, George worked in McKinley National Park with Gordon Haber, a doctoral candidate who was studying wild wolves. In the field, George observed breeding and hunting patterns of the wolf pack. She recorded it all in her notebooks. Back in New York, George consulted her editor, Andy Jones, then went home to write. A week later Jones phoned to cancel the piece. There had been a mistake: in her absence, another wolf article had been purchased. Crushed, George reorganized her notes and phoned her daughter to discuss the demise of her project. At the core of her discomfort was the debt of obligation she felt to the scientists. "Why don't you write a children's book about wolves?" suggested her daughter.

The very next day, sitting across the desk from Ursula Nordstrom, George explained her idea. "I want to write a book about an Eskimo girl who is lost on the Arctic tundra. She survives by communicating with a pack of wolves in their own language."

"Will it be accurate?"

"Yes."

The sketches and notes accumulated in her Arctic notebooks assured the scientific accuracy of *Julie of the Wolves*. George's artistry created the story. "My journal isn't good reading," says George. "It's really putting things down to help me find the story and the poetry in the story . . . and to conjure up images in my mind. I close my eyes, open them and begin to write."

Jean Craighead George's books include

Julie of the Wolves
Julie's Wolfpack
My Side of the Mountain
One Day in the Tropical Forest
Everglades
The Tarantula in My Purse

The Interview

From the age of ten I kept a diary every day. My family was always respectful of it and nobody ever read it. In college my emphasis shifted as I made my diary more of a journal.

Because I can't remember everything, I find a journal a wonderful place to refresh visions and names and places. I even make sketches in my journal so I can go back to the setting. It's a pivotal point: I open it and I'm back where I was. I'm refreshed and can move around from there. When I wrote my autobiography, *Journey Inward*, I went back over all my journals.

Source Book

Today my journals, which are 6-by-9-inch secretarial notebooks, are reference books for my professional writing, combining research notes and personal observations. I'm usually writing two or three books at the same time, and I have a separate notebook for each one. The first note, dated October 26, 1992, in the *There's An Owl in the Shower* notebook is about how animal populations are distributed patchily in nature. That's certainly true for the spotted owl. I have formulas written down and notes from people who were talking about the distributions of population.

Next I have notes from a trip to the spruce forest where the spotted owl lives. I've listed the plants: sorrel, huckleberry, red

From Jean Craighead George's sketchbook for *Water Sky*

huckleberry, and stinging nettles. From a walk with my son Luke in the Redwood National Park I list the trees with their Latin names as well as their popular ones. It was a breathtaking walk among giant trees along Lady Bird Johnson's Redwood Trail. In great big letters I wrote I SAW AN ALBINO ROBIN. I also saw controlled burning on a hillside in the park and I made note of that.

This, like all my notebooks, is a rather jerky combination of observations, sketches, notes, and quotes. "October 28: two fishermen on the rocks, two marsh hawks chasing a redtail hawk over the grassland." Back at my son's home I sketched the pine siskins and dark-eyed juncos that came to his feeder. Following the personal observations there is information from the U.S. Forest Service and a lovely quote from one man, "There is no stability in nature." Then a diagram about why the spotted owl is declining. They must have giant trees because they must nest up high where the atmosphere is right for their young. It can't be too wet, too dry, too hot or cold. I have a map of the forest which shows islands of giant trees where the spotted owl

nests. But the areas around these little islands of trees have been cut and logged, and spotted owls can't get together.

Emergence of the Story

After making my notes and sketches the story evolves. While I was camping in the forest I saw for myself that the owls are isolated and can't hear each other. This tragic fact turns out to be very important to my book.

I go on to the Willow Creek Study Area where Chris Moen shows me a spotted owl nest. Chris makes the call of the spotted owl and out flies a beautiful male. She holds up a mouse and the owl carries it off into a tree where it swallows it whole and sits there, only forty feet from us, totally unafraid and unconcerned. This bird, I learned, was called Enrico. He becomes the father owl in my book. In the morning he goes back to his tree to roost. It's right above a lumber road. As he sits there during the day the dust from the road spins into the air and settles over him until he looks more like a red owl than a spotted owl. I stand and watch him.

The story builds with information from books I'm reading: notes from William Dietrich's *The Final Forest*, a fabulous book on the Pacific forests; notes from a book about the life cycle of the spotted owl. I go over these notes for ideas. Eggs are laid in April, hatch in May. In June the female forages and stays with the babies until they have enough feathers to survive, about six weeks. And there are clippings, many articles from newspapers. I've also noted that the territory of the Northern spotted owl is two hundred thousand acres. All of this information becomes part of the story.

From Notebook to Book

When I heard about the demise of the spotted owl and the position of the lumbermen resulting in the fight for the big trees out west, I was enchanted. I thought, "I've got to write this story, but how do I present both sides?" I went into the forest, took notes and personal observations, read about the spotted owl and the battle between loggers and environmentalists, drew diagrams, sketched trees and wildlife. My story emerged from my journal, which is the important reason to keep notes. A journal does this for you.

Having absorbed all of this information and seeing the story, I sat down to write. Going back to childhood diaries, I realized we kept owls as kids. If you get them young, as we always did, they imprint on you. They would cuddle under our chins, sit on our shoulders. They thought that we were their mothers so they would hop along behind us, ride on our bike handles, take showers with us—that's where the title *There's an Owl in the Shower* came from. The book is about an owl who imprints on a tough old lumberman and thinks he's its parent.

Works in Progress

When I'm researching a story, I write in my journal and sketch as part of my daily routine. I use Japanese prayer books for sketching because I can keep pulling out the paper and draw huge panoramic scenes. I take one of those books with me wherever I go.

When I went to the Arctic to research *Water Sky* I drew scenes of people whaling—everybody standing on the ice, people pulling in the whale, the camps and tents and the vast sea of ice. After being out on that sea of ice I knew what thirty-five below zero feels like.

I talked to the Eskimos and bought their publications from the town hall. The North Slope Planning Commission was a rich source of cultural material—stories from the old Eskimos, information about their dances, music, drums, customs. I carried a backpack of books home. More notes.

My journal isn't good reading. It's really putting things down to help me find the story and the poetry in the story—words like Douglas fir, rhododendron—and to conjure up images in my mind. I close my eyes, open them, and begin to write.

Bits and Pieces

It's tough for kids to get started on journal keeping, so I suggest they bring back little things they pick up along their ways—folders from the Museum of Natural History, a leaf, a dandelion—and paste them into a notebook. Then they can write their thoughts about them, what they saw and what they felt. It's a beginning, a way to get started, as I do when I list the trees and birds I observe out in nature. My notes motivate me to write a story, and theirs might do the same for them.

Jim Arnosky

"Looking, Watching, Wondering"

Naturalist Jim Arnosky has made a career of inciting children to delight in their natural world. He worries that advances in technology—punching a keyword into a computer and displaying a thousand entries—will separate children from life's actual, tactile experiences. To him, the smallest personal experience overshadows the most extravagant and most beautifully written account.

Arnosky writes only from direct observation and personal experience. Going outdoors into nature sometimes with no more than a spiral notebook and a number 2 pencil in his shirt pocket, he makes his living doing what he loves most—watching, wondering about, and sketching wildlife.

An old beekeeper first encouraged Arnosky to start keeping a journal. Forced by a stroke to sell his equipment and quit a wondrous way of life, the old man regretted not taking time to record the colorful experiences he'd enjoyed while keeping bees and selling honey. Arnosky took this advice to heart. A leather-bound sketch book, with a ribbon page marker, became his outdoor companion. He took it everywhere: canoeing, fishing, following moose tracks through the forest. Considering himself primarily an artist, Arnosky expected he would be sketching, but he also found himself recording his reflections about wildlife. More than 4,000 pages later, his journal, which he compares to a vessel, contains his first-hand observations. Most written entries are illustrated, each captioned with a title and date. Arnosky writes only when he has something to say. Two months may go by without an entry; then, if he's seen a bear, he might fill four pages.

A self-confessed compulsive animal tracker, Arnosky rambles the countryside on snowshoes, reading the stories animals write on fresh snowfalls. Twice a year, once in the fall and again in the winter, he climbs the hills behind his Vermont farmhouse to survey the wide expanse of scenery. The view thrills him, but makes him eager to get closer to a setting in which he finds his place in the natural order of the world—outdoors, close to the earth and water, near the birds and beasts. Becoming part of this scene, he is more aware of his immediate surroundings.

"Like a raccoon ambling down a streambed," Arnosky writes in *Nearer Nature*, "my focus is on the close-up details." Children, he says, live inside scenery; adults try to buy the scene. Arnosky, who has never outgrown his childhood perspective, relishes following the dainty footprints of a fox and observing the wanderings of a winter stone fly.

Through his books and television shows Arnosky invites children to become curious wildlife watchers with him. He stimulates them to keep an eye out for the smallest details and make outdoor discoveries of their own. In *Secrets of a Wildlife Watcher*, he urges readers to pay attention to particulars, to ponder what they see—not just look, but observe—to keep a wildlife notebook and record their findings. Arnosky also shares practical tips for successful wildlife stalking: keep still, stay downwind, disguise your human shape by crouching down. He encourages readers to collect their own secrets about wildlife spaces, hiding places, and patterns of behavior and to pass them along to a friend.

For Arnosky, there is little distinction between work and leisure. He finds no difference between weekdays and weekends. The activities of the animals he chooses to study set his daily schedule. He spends most of his days roaming the woods near his home, observing and sketching wildlife.

For the past twenty years, Arnosky and his family have lived in a 160-year-old farmhouse on fifty-one acres of land. Their house, barn, and woodshed are tucked back against mountains, away from traffic and the noise of the villages. They have grown their own vegetables and flowers, kept bees for sweets, and raised sheep. "In this old house," writes Arnosky in the introduction to *Nearer Nature*, "I organize my thoughts and record them in my journals."

Jim Arnosky's books include

Secrets of a Wildlife Watcher
Drawing from Nature
Crinkleroot's Nature Almanac
Watching Water Birds
Watching Desert Wildlife
Nearer Nature (for adults)

The Interview

When I was twenty-six I decided I wanted to keep bees. I didn't know a thing about it, but I had seen an ad in the paper for the equipment, so I thought I would go by. It turned out to be a sweet, elderly man who had kept bees for sixty years. He had had a stroke and had to stop. He couldn't remember anything about his life as a beekeeper. The only way he could piece together his knowledge of this wonderful way of life—keeping bees, selling honey—was to look at all his receipts. He was remorseful that he hadn't sat down every week and written what had transpired. "Do yourself a favor," he told me. "Keep a journal." I took him to heart.

I got into bee keeping and it was part of my life—raising a garden for food and honey for sweets. Later, sheep. I didn't keep meticulous notes unless it involved something I was doing wrong or when the bees would chase me. In the beginning, I kept a record of the learning curve.

Around the same time, I bought a nice leather-bound notebook. Since I thought of myself as an artist, I decided to keep a sketch book. I took it with me in the canoe and everywhere I went. I found myself sketching, but also writing, mostly reflections about my observations of wildlife. Today, in a total of sixteen leather-bound journals, I have easily over 4,000 pages. Most are illustrated entries, each captioned with a title and date. Since I write only when I am thinking clearly about what I want to record, my journal is free of muddled thoughts and misgivings. I write when I have something to say. If I've seen a bear, I'll come home and write four pages. Sometimes whole months go by with no entry; sometimes I'm writing every day.

Fishing Log

Fishing became a way for me to be outdoors and be unobtrusive and observe wildlife while they weren't concerned about me. Many of my greatest wildlife observations come from times when I was busy fishing. Wild animals are as attentive to their particular environments as humans are. An animal knows when you are interested in it, as opposed to your walking by or just being there. When you are fishing, the wildlife knows you are not interested in them, per se. You are not part of their sphere of concern.

My journal has many fishing entries. One day, for example, I was busy tying a fly to my line when a cedar waxwing perched on the tip of the pole. It had been flying across a wide expanse of water and decided to use my fishing pole to rest. There I was with a bird at the top of my fishing pole acting as if it could care less if I was there. It wasn't threatened because I was busy doing something else.

Wildlife Journal

In 1987 after I finished the PBS series "Drawing from Nature,"

I took a hiatus from work and decided to go out each day and simply enjoy nature. It was a tonic for me to take the time away from my own requirements of always asking, "What am I going to do with this information?" I just let nature flow into me and onto the pages of my journal. In those seven months I learned so much more about the landscape, and by adhering to a rigorous schedule I found myself drawing nearer and nearer to the animals.

From January to July of that year, I would walk the same route every morning and every afternoon and every evening. I did it daily and for its own sake. I based my one-mile hike on the path my cats took from the barn to the woods to the cove, along the river, through a meadow, and then back home. I figured if it kept them healthy and hardy, it should be good enough for me. That's how I ended up being able to observe the same animals constantly. I followed a routine because animals live within a routine, but no day was typical.

After seven months, it was hard for me to continue without

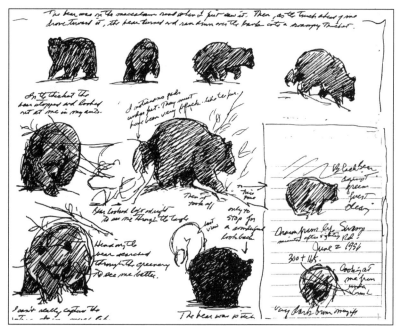

Sketches from Jim Arnosky's journal

sharing. If you're a miser you can become sickly. If you share, you're wealthy. I have a rich life, and if I hoard my experiences, it makes me feel less good about my life. I've had the chance to live in a way many people haven't had the opportunity to do. I felt that it was worth trying to take what was in those journal pages and make it into a book. Thoreau had written _Walden_ from his journal. But he also lived fairly close to his mom's home and was in a position to go home and get away from his experiment at Walden Pond. In my case, I was just living my life. I wasn't going back to anything. My wife and I are here. This is us. So far, _Nearer Nature_ is the only one of my books drawn completely from my journals.

Animal Tracker

I had signed a contract to write a book about sketching in autumn, and I didn't want to write a book about the things people usually think of. One night, on my way home from fishing, a bull moose stepped in front of me. The next day I went back and found its tracks. This is not a tall tale: I followed the tracks for twenty-five days and found things to sketch along the way. (Of course, I returned home each evening.) The moose led me through all the places in the forest that I would never go, because I wouldn't know where to go. After twenty-five days I found the moose again and sketched it from life. I wrote a song about it, which I'm illustrating now, a comical version. It was just something that happened, and I felt very fortunate that I was the person it happened to.

Fieldwork

I was a wildlife photographer at age nineteen and managed to support myself and my interest in illustration. I never had any art lessons, didn't go to college, and never had art in grade school. I decided to take time off to teach myself to draw many things I never knew how to draw, outside of cartooning, which I was doing quite well. I wrote a book called _Drawing from Nature_ that led to a PBS television series in 1986. During the production of the series, I became fascinated with the video equipment. I started using video in the field to capture the movement of animals.

Then I went through another period when I wanted to brush up on my abilities as an illustrator. I put away all the camera equipment and sketched for three straight years. Instead of going into the field with a camera, I took my sketchbook. Now I double. I'm always dipping into video and learning how to do even better in using it for wildlife observations. If I feel the need to get better at something—landscape, for example—I'll take a year and do nothing but landscape sketches. When you are self-taught, you have to go by your own indicators.

Pocket Notebook and Number 2 Pencil

When it comes to video, I love equipment. When it comes to drawing, I never learned anything about supplies. If I had to figure out what kind of paper and what kind of pencil and what medium I was going to work in, I'd never have gotten anything done. I've made an entire living with a number 2 pencil. I draw as fast as I can see. I have sketched animals dashing away from me and swimming away from me. I never use an eraser. I just draw. If I make a mistake I keep drawing over it and over it until it looks right.

I carry a little notebook and a pen or pencil in my pocket all the time. When I come home I tape those pages into the journal. I believe there's nothing more beautiful than an original sketch. I've never been able to duplicate in the second draft of a drawing the original quality of the first.

Living Inside the Scene

The real skill in journal keeping is to make yourself the key character in all the entries while still managing to write a journal that is not about you. Children live inside scenery; adults want somehow to buy the view. Many people admire sunsets while fishing from their boats and immediately picture the scene on a calendar. When we are children, we are the scenery. I have never grown out of that. I always reflect myself in the scene. I'd much rather be in the hills, walking through the mist following a storm, than in a house looking out the window at the hills.

Thinking is not a replacement for living. I don't like nurturing the concept in children that if they read about an eagle, it somehow equals seeing one. I'm always hopeful that teachers and parents will stress the importance of the smallest personal experience over the most extravagant and most beautifully written account of something. My life experiences surpass everything I've ever read. You don't have to be an expert to have valid observations and experiences. I'm just a regular guy who grew up wanting to be Davy Crockett. And because I put value in my own experiences and observation, I now know there are youngsters who want to grow up to be Jim Arnosky.

The tremendous access children have to information worries me. They can sit at a computer and punch up 38,000 entries about rattlesnakes. I know having an experience with a real rattlesnake overshadows everything I could see on a computer screen. I believe that the tactile world becomes more and more important as our mental and communication abilities advance. The faster and more rapid these things advance, the more important the actual experience of the world becomes. Life cannot be reading about or writing about life. Living life is what counts, with or without the journal.

Kathleen Krull

"It Keeps You off the Street"

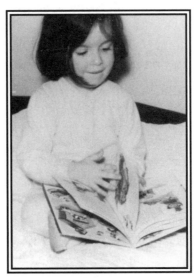

Kathleen Krull, a reader
since age 5

Kathleen Krull is such a passionate advocate of journal keeping that she sometimes reads from her sixth-grade diary at author appearances.

Sixth grade, April 20: "Today I went on my first "DATE" with Raymond (John Timothy) Kehoe to Parker's across the street from school. I had a Cherry Coke. He paid. HILARIOUS."

Sixth grade, April 28: "He asked me again. I went. We went with Paul Koller, and Susan Hall (the latest pair!) it was a ball! . . . I'm beginning to like him a whole lot but it's getting harder to give excuses to my parents! Cruel parents! There's nothing wrong with Parker's either (or with Raymond)! Bye for now — your creator — Kathy Krull"

Krull's excursions into journal keeping took a detour in junior high, but in the eighth grade she wrote her first short story, a horror tale titled "Death Waits Until After Dark." Her teacher thought the story was mean-spirited and unbelievable, but she gave Krull an A anyway, because she liked the writing. This same teacher was the first person to encourage Krull to consider becoming a professional writer. Krull later enrolled at Lawrence University in Appleton, Wisconsin, majoring in English, with writing assignments nudging personal writing to the bottom of the stack.

During her subsequent ten-year career in publishing, Krull resumed writing in her trusty diary, now a typewritten journal, and since the age of twenty-two she has written in it almost daily. Shortly after leaving publishing, Krull had a dream, duly recorded in her journal, about a collection of hymns for children. *Songs of Praise* became her first book published as a freelance writer. Recurring nightmares, which she also recorded in her journals, led to the creation of her chapter book *Alex Fitzgerald's Cure for Nightmares* and its sequel *Alex Fitzgerald, TV Star*.

Not all of her books, she notes, spring so directly from her diary. To ascertain direction from within—determine where to focus her energies, which genre to pursue, when to change course if a project isn't going well—Krull consults her journal. When she was writing *V is for Victory*, for example, Krull noticed that she was recording constant, unusual headaches. She finally linked the headaches to the fact that she was writing daily about the different ways millions of people had died during World War II. Krull decided to avoid taking on such weighty issues in the future.

Celebrating her hobbies and often quirky fascinations in her journals has led Krull to write intriguing biographies of famous people. Her curiosity about psychics, for example, inspired *They Saw the Future: Oracles, Psychics, Scientists, Great Thinkers and Pretty Good Guessers*. In *Lives of the Musicians: Good Times, Bad Times (And What the Neighbors Thought)* as well as in its four companions about artists, writers, athletes, and presidents, Krull fuses personal passions—music, strong women, how fame affects people—into her professional writing. Critics have praised her ability to animate standard, straightforward biographical information with offbeat details and amusing anecdotes. By revealing the human side of legendary figures, she encourages children's interests in the lives of famous people.

In her journal, Krull pays close attention to her use of language as well as to what is unique about herself. She experiments with forms of expression and talks to herself as an editor would as she slogs through revisions. More than a friend, her journal has become the operating manual for her writing career. She makes choices about future projects and tries to regain her sense of humor after "stinging rejections, disgusting first drafts, bad reviews . . . and other trials."

Now, after thousands of pages, Krull openly admits an addiction to journal writing. She doesn't apologize. "It's hard to define, but I know intuitively that a journal is essential for my professional life. I couldn't do what I do if I didn't keep one."

With limitless curiosity and interests, Kathleen Krull could easily lose herself in a maze of possibility, but using her journal as compass, she finds true north in a career that comes with no maps and no bosses to tell her what to do.

Kathleen Krull's books include

Lives of the Presidents: Fame, Shame (And What the Neighbors Thought)
Lives of the Musicians: Good Times, Bad Times (And What the Neighbors Thought)
Wilma Unlimited: How Wilma Rudolph Became the World's Fastest Woman
They Saw the Future: Oracles, Psychics, Scientists, Great Thinkers and Pretty Good Guessers
Alex Fitzgerald's Cure for Nightmares
Wish You Were Here: Emily's Guide to the 50 States

The Interview

When I turned ten, either my mother or grandmother gave me a pink, leather-bound diary with its own lock and key. I was too busy living life, or maybe I didn't yet grasp the concept— it didn't come with instructions! But during my entire fifth grade year I pencilled in a total of three entries. When sixth grade rolled around I still had this mostly blank book. I've always liked to recycle, so I erased what I had written in fifth grade and just started over.

Sixth grade was a big year. I had a crush on Mr. Banks, my teacher, as well as on a boy in my class, Raymond. I still didn't have the knack of writing every day, so I would pop in once in a while and bring the reader up to date. I wrote about going to the library with my mom and checking out stacks of "real good books," having fights with my moody girlfriends, arguing with my brothers, getting in lots of trouble for being too giddy, receiving lectures from both my parents on being a lady. I neglected to mention JFK's assassination that year or indeed any other event beyond my own tiny, but slowly expanding world. Then I lost the hang of diaries completely and didn't keep one in seventh or eighth grade.

In high school I had a lot to say, and I needed a lot of diaries. My freshman year I filled four diaries covered in fake leopard skin. My sophomore year burst the seams of a fat green diary. Discovering the manual typewriter when I was 16 was like the "Star Wars" shift into hyperspeed for me. I stopped writing by hand and began a new adventure called a journal. Ambitiously, pompously, I called it "Reveries: A Journal of Incidents, Insight, Impressions, and Illusions with Illustrations by the Author."

Journal Snoops

I had three younger brothers who were most curious about my diaries. I went to great lengths to hide or disguise them. It didn't matter. My next oldest brother would snoop through my things, pick the locks, do whatever he had to do. To prove that he'd been successful at invading my sacred space, he'd write snide commentary in my diary, giving away the fact that he'd read it. He should have become a detective when he grew up.

I was furious, not just at the invasion, but also at how powerless I felt. My parents didn't take the crime as seriously as I thought they should, and I could tell they thought my plight was kind of funny. Eventually my brother got a life and stopped bugging me, but I never felt completely secure about expressing personal thoughts until I moved out of the house and went to college in another state.

Since then, I don't think I've had any snoopers. A few times I've chosen to share certain entries with people in my life, usually during an impasse in the relationship, when I'm hoping to make my point of view clearer. This almost always backfires— I end up inadvertently hurting the person's feelings and making things worse. Once I let a troubled 14-year-old read my leopard-skin diaries, hoping she would find comfort in my angst at that age. This gesture backfired too. She called me "pathetic." I couldn't argue, but I also couldn't get her to see the point that out of such pathos a reasonably functional adult can emerge.

Most ironically, I now use my early diaries in school presentations—no privacy there. Sometimes at bookstores, I read from my sixth grade diary and in general hype diaries so much that kids, instead of buying my books, buy new diaries and have me sign them. This year I even had my brother in the audience during a presentation. Who could imagine I'd one day be reading my diaries aloud right in front of him!

Back in the Groove

I graduated from Lawrence University in Wisconsin, majoring in English, minoring in music. My career goal was to be a writer. I was doing so much writing for classes that I backpedaled on my journal keeping. It was a case of real life being overwhelming, and it seemed more important to live it than to write it. I did get obsessed with Virginia Woolf and spent much time immersed in her stimulating diaries. After college there were those immediate problems of rent and bills. I went to work for a publishing company because I couldn't see any way of generating income with my own words. But I was addicted to writing, and not having the outlet for it like I did in college, I resumed my trusty journal. Ever since I was twenty-one or twenty-two, I have written in it almost every day. I switched over to keeping it on a computer about ten years ago, and long ago stopped illustrating it. This is where I try to make sense of my life, to observe the world around me and comment.

I don't think I would be a writer if it weren't for the journal. I worked in publishing as an editor for over ten years, and then I felt the need for a break. I decided to lounge around the beach in California and see what thoughts came to me (hoping they'd come quick, before my money ran out). I figured I'd end up getting another job in publishing and moving back to the Midwest. I kept track of my thoughts and feelings in my journal, and finally I realized that I wanted to stay where I was and write. With that new focus, suddenly ideas for books began popping into my head. My journal was acting like a compass, pointing me in the direction that was right for me.

Daily Warm-up

Journal-writing is the first thing I do in the morning, sipping Earl Grey tea mixed with a little milk. If I don't catch my thoughts right away, they evaporate into the energy of the tasks at hand for that day, never to be retrieved. I begin by recording dreams, a habit I started in high school. Initially I thought of taking the wispy, non-verbal threads of dreams and translating them into words on a page as a challenge, a useful writing exercise. I notice recurring themes, insights into waking life, psychic premonitions, things that frighten me into nightmares. Over time, I've gotten several ideas for books from dreams and am always figuring out ways of solving writing problems and making choices. As one example, during a period when I was having a lot of nightmares, I wrote *Alex Fitzgerald's Cure for Nightmares* out of my own experience.

I'm totally addicted to journal writing and can't imagine what would ever stop me. But I think it's important not to get obsessed and let it take over real life. I limit myself to twenty minutes to a half hour. It's my warm-up for the rest of the day, a way of getting into the groove of shaping messy thoughts into coherent words. It's been a place for me to experiment with being witty and concise, putting things in an entertaining way, mixing amusing gossip with weighty thoughts. Sometimes reviewers comment on my conversational style—I worked out this style in my journal. I try not to be boring. Instead, I try to pay attention to what's unique about my use of language, using combinations of words only I would use. A journal is a cheap

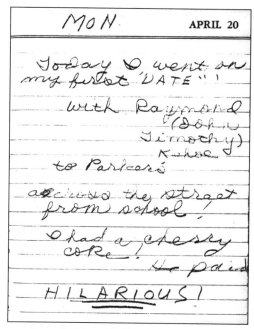

From Kathleen Krull's sixth-grade diary

writing teacher. It's a way to give myself feedback on my own work as I'm going along in my endless revisions.

When I'm traveling or away from my desk in the morning, I prefer to observe what's going on and not distract myself by taking notes. What if I miss something? But the next chance I get, I sit down at the computer and gather impressions from the previous days and shape them into words. I'm consciously trying to develop my powers of recall and to bring alive something that's already happened. It's a way to improve my memory skills, which have always been weak.

I keep the entries organized by month on my hard drive. I'll take them off every so often and store them on a disk that goes into a drawer. I'm a procrastinator about printing it out, and it usually takes two years or more. I keep the printed copy in big black binders on a shelf. I have thousands of pages.

Brutal Honesty

The motto "know thyself" is important for everyone and especially for writers or artists. There are so many choices and variables to your existence that it's crucial to determine your true feelings. Censoring what I write would miss the whole point. Even when I knew my brother was snooping, I would be brutally honest in whatever I wrote. I'm not cryptic. It seems silly to me to falsify things or make them up in a journal. I analyze events and people as truthfully as I can. I want to know what these things mean. Otherwise, why bother?

True North

Writers don't have typical supports that other people do. It's life in a vacuum. We have only words to work with—no visuals or other sensory aids, no office staff to commiserate with, no bosses to say "good job" or "bad job," no way of ascertaining direction except from within ourselves. Everything about this life is trial and error, there are no maps. But keeping a journal can act like a compass, helping you get your bearings.

I can't count the ways keeping a journal is good for you. Mainly, it satisfies deep emotional needs—a desire for order, the need for help in making choices, a craving to see into the future, the need for comfort during stressful times, the drive to develop vision and wisdom, the urge to get help in the lifelong pursuit of understanding oneself and one's place in the universe. It is so odd to think that writing things down—one step above talking to yourself, really—can help with all this, but it does, mysteriously.

It's hard to define, but I know intuitively that a journal is essential for my professional life. I just couldn't do what I do if I didn't keep one. It's where I analyze how a project is going— am I feeling confident, or would I be better off changing gears? I've been able to determine who are and who are not my true friends in helping my writing. I keep track of books I'm reading and analyze them. This is where I nurse myself back to strength after stinging rejections, disgusting first drafts, bad reviews, mean editors, jealousy of other writers, laughable royalty checks, and other trials.

This is also the place where I ask myself: what next? It has really helped with the notion of knowing myself and where to focus my energies. I find out that a particular project or genre may not be right for me, or it may be something I dearly love. I know from my journal, for example, that I'm happiest when writing fiction. But I also know that, lacking a trust fund, writing nonfiction is how I make my living.

Journal Disaster

A few years back I tried to fit too many months of the journal on a disk, and the disk exploded. I had lost a year and a half of gossip! This boyfriend of a good friend of mine was a computer expert who said that sometimes data gone bad could be recovered. I was so agitated at the thought of losing all that material that I gladly turned my sacred disk over to this guy. Too late I recalled that lately I'd been writing numerous biting comments about this very person. I could only pray that he was so much of a computer nerd that he would have no curiosity about what the disk contained. He never said, and I'll never know. He was able to recover about two-thirds of the disk, and the rest was gone forever. I did mourn losing my record of a big trip to New York. I had taken careful notes of conversations with editors. This was important enough to me to go back and try to reconstruct. But otherwise it seemed a sign of serious neurosis to write the journal twice. I tried to be philosophical about the rest and move on—the journal had fulfilled its purpose at the time; so what if I had lost a few months?

Ten Bits of Advice for Journal Keepers

1. Don't come down on yourself too hard if you find you're not too faithful.
2. Don't come down on yourself too hard if you find you're spending eight hours a day at it. Writing about yourself can be addictive.
3. Try to keep it in a safe place.
4. Training yourself to think by putting your thoughts into words is incredibly valuable even if you don't want to be a writer when you grow up. You will be surprised to find out just how many jobs require words. But a journal is the single most important thing you can do if you think you do want to be a writer. For one thing, this is a bottomless gold mine of material—you never know what books your messy life will inspire.
5. You'll always have a record of what you experienced, the things you thought were important, the secrets you had, even if it's a haphazard account. When you're a rich and famous celebrity, you'll also have the outline for your memoirs.
6. It teaches you about language and about yourself.
7. It keeps you from watching too much TV.
8. It's a valuable part of living. For one thing, it acts like a

secret psychic by helping you make choices that influence your future.

9. It helps to slow time down and let you experience each moment. Eventually you will find that letting life fly by unanalyzed is really disturbing.

10. It keeps you off the street.

Mary Jane Miller

"More than Words on Paper"

Mary Jane Miller as a schoolgirl

Mary Jane Miller finds shelter in her journal. It's the safe harbor she visits when tossed about by the currents of life. Here she ties up to seek solace and guidance, to reflect on the writing process, to ponder her life as a fiction writer, to ask and answer questions.

During her childhood, she says, books were as important to her as food. Reading eventually led her to journal writing, a practice that has sustained her for nearly twenty-five years. Browsing the library shelves on a summer afternoon in 1976, Miller discovered Madeleine L'Engle's *Crosswicks Journals*. Immersing herself in these volumes inspired Miller to begin her own personal journal. In the early days, this mother of four daughters recorded the flow of life, be it joyful, sad, or mundane.

Twenty-seven journals, tucked away on a shelf in her study closet, attest to Miller's faithful recording of the minutiae of everyday domestic life. Recently, however, she has shifted course. In a sustained inner dialogue with her journals as guide, she explores the uncharted waters of her subconscious.

Miller began her writing career in the 1970s and found ready acceptance in magazines, newsletters, and newspapers. Answering the question "What does one do with the crumbs in the bottom of the cookie jar?" her first sale was a household hint to *Family Circle*. Acceptance reinforced her dream of becoming a professional writer, and she went on to publish how-to articles and teen profiles in *Seventeen*. She also wrote feature articles for local newspapers, all the while hungering for fiction sales.

Into her journal she poured her longing to be accepted as a writer and recorded the stinging pain of rejection. Finally, in 1989 Miller's novel *Me and My Name* was purchased by Viking. She celebrated in her journal: "VIKING SAID YES! THANK YOU! THANK YOU!" Three middle-grade novels followed quickly, after which a lull in acceptances took her toward a deeper level of journal writing.

Today, Miller writes in three journals simultaneously: a gratitude journal, a reflection notebook, and a question journal. She takes stock of the things for which she is grateful and finds that by simply listing those items, she creates a log of her day.

In the reflection notebook she meditates on lines by authors, wise sayings by Vietnamese monk Thich Nhat Hanh, for example, and ponders her writing process.

In her question journal, Miller asks, "How does one cultivate happiness? Does God understand? What is my heart whispering? What is my spiritual symbol? What do you do when you're stuck in the sand on a lazy, stubborn camel?" She finds she is constantly surprised by what appears on the pages of these journals.

"You know you're not going to spend the day writing in your journal, so the subconscious chooses for you," she says. She trusts her inner guide to help her examine "the scars that ache on a rainy day" as well as to encourage her to face inhibitions, stare down her inner critic, and develop a deep awareness of the natural beauty that surrounds her.

At this stage of life, Mary Jane Miller is exploring her story-telling heritage, which is deeply rooted in the land of the ancient Celts. She draws on the legacy of her Irish grandmother who spun marvelous tales while reading tea leaves. She writes for that eleven-, twelve-, thirteen-year-old child who is still a part of her. While she confesses uncertainty about how her journal writing nourishes her fiction, Miller's inner searching links directly to the concerns of young readers who need to know who they are and where they fit in.

And what does one do with the cookie crumbs? "You mix them with brown sugar, a little cinnamon, and make a topping for the fresh coffee cake you just baked."

Mary Jane Miller's books include

Me and My Name
Upside Down
Fast Forward
Going the Distance

The Interview

My first journal entry is dated September 4, 1976. It is a page and a half entry written in pencil that has begun to fade. I ask myself a question on this first page. "Where am I going with my willy-nilly reading?" I answer my own question. "To writing, I hope."

Reading brought me to journal writing. While browsing through the library shelves one summer afternoon, I found Madeleine L'Engle's *Crosswick Journals*. Reading Madeleine's books inspired, encouraged, and led me to keeping a journal.

Today on a shelf in my study closet there are twenty-seven journals. Nineteen of them are arranged by date. The dated ones record daily living, thoughts, feelings, and poetry. The other journals record vacations, spiritual wanderings, insights, prayers, quotations, and reflections on the process of writing.

Changes

For the past year I have been keeping a gratitude journal. And to my surprise, I no longer record daily living. The need to write in my other journals outweighs the need to record each day.

There are other changes. In the beginning, like an accountant, I used ledger books with black covers. Now I look for a cover with flowers, an unusual design, something that draws me to a particular journal. My handwriting has changed. It's less cramped and now there are flourishes.

Everyday Notations

Often in my journal writing I write about what a moment evokes.

March 15, 1997: Walking to the hospital to see Dad, I stopped on the bridge that crosses the Chicago River. The river was green in anticipation of St. Patrick's Day. The wind blew my hair and for that minute I felt alive and very young.

Sunday, December 29, 1996: Yesterday, viewing the Degas exhibit was a wondrous and wonderful experience. I felt called to the painting and was delighted to read that Degas discovered a whole new way of painting when he was past fifty. It was as if Degas spoke to me: move forward. Reach out. Change. Grow. There's time.

Drawing from the Journal

On occasion I go back and reread my journals, and while I don't translate the material directly into fiction, I draw on it.

Undated Journal Entry: In Monterey, Leanne, Joe and I walked along the beach, a promise fulfilled. In my mind's eye, I will always see Leanne with her jeans rolled up, barefoot, long blond hair glistening in the sun, delighting in the waves one minute, and the next minute, Leanne struggling as she was being swept away by the force of the undertow. Joe reached her and carried her back to shore. Now she is sleeping after a warm bath and much comforting. I will be forever grateful.

When I was writing *Me and My Name* this scene returned to my consciousness. I remembered Leanne's need for comfort and how much she needed my arms around her. In the scene I was writing, Erin had to acknowledge the conflicting emotions she was feeling. And so Erin walks the beach in Florida with her biological father, Paul. A wave rolls in and knocks Erin down. More waves sweep over her. What happened to Leanne became a part of Erin's reality. In *Me and My Name* I wrote: "It was warm and cozy sitting next to Daddy, but I wanted Mom. And I wanted one of Leo's bear hugs."

More Than Words on Paper

The process of journal writing is also a pathway to the subconscious, a way for me to discover who I am.

March 24, 1993: A new journal _____ blank pages. Reflection. Writing the words—words of life, as lived, perceived, thought and felt.

March 1989 [before *Me and My Name* was published]:
Damp dark day. A nesting day. I sit here in my study, my ivory tower and feel cozy. Yesterday a poem popped into my head. Have to put it to paper before it disappears.

"QUESTIONS"

I never question
the fact
that my eyes are blue.
And I've never once questioned
my silver hair.

I've never questioned
the gender
female.
So why do I ask
am I a writer?

Joy is painted on paper.

May 19, 1989, across the pages of my journal, in capital letters: VIKING SAID YES! THANK YOU! THANK YOU!

Memory is crystallized.

May 22, 1989: The moment when Jane [my agent, Jane Jordan Browne] called and asked, how would you like to be published by Viking? is crystallized in my memory. Me—standing in the kitchen—wearing old blue shorts and a T-shirt talking to Joe. The phone ringing. The gasp! The shriek! The tears! The joy, the wondrous, marvelous, mountain-moving joy. To know that the path is the right path!

Moments of reflection.

February 22, 1990: Just finished reviewing the copy-editing of *Me and My Name*. How strange it is to read a story, like it and know that it came from deep inside of you. Interesting thought: Paul, who is Erin's biological father is a photojournalist. Is that the part of me that longs for far away places? Something to think about.

Now, seven years later I have taken up photography. Something more to think about.

My journal records our family history, as Joe and I and our daughters journey through the years.

July 1978: Cloudy. July 12. We are on vacation at last. The kids were a big help in getting us here. Bowers. A pocket of peace. Everyone is still sleeping so I have a few minutes to myself. Hard to believe the kids are growing up so quickly and yet they still squabble in the car. The latest expression is "squish brain."
1990 (twelve years later): How strange is the moment when you truly see your children as adults. My babies are women! How can this be? You look back and realize how quickly the days, the years slip by. But I wouldn't go back. Being Mom has new dimensions now. I am also friend and confidant.

In 1986 our dog Buttons, who was part of our family for fourteen years, died. I was able to express my grief in my journal.

1986: Buttons, Ba is gone. Our silly old dog with a heart full of love for everyone but magazine sales people slipped away this morning. How quiet the house is and yet her presence is still felt. I told the kids energy never dies, it changes form. Buttons' spirit will be with us forever.

And she is. As a family, we still tell tales of Ba. "Remember when Buttons ate all the cupcakes and the paper? Remember how she'd hide in the bathtub when it thundered?"

Too Close to the Bone

There have been times when I have been unable to write anything in my journal. In 1977, my mother-in-law and my father both died, suddenly, within three weeks of each other. At that time there were no words to express my grief. Twelve years later I wrote:

> December 16, 1989: Last night, so close to Christmas, to Dad's birthday, we gathered together in front of the fire and shared memories of Dad (Papa). Early this morning I searched my 1977 journal seeking to find what I had written, my thoughts and feelings. Nothing but facts! Too close to the bone, I guess, but now after much time has passed, I can remember and write. The thoughts, feelings and questions will make their way into a book.

And they did. In my second book, *Upside Down,* the first sentence of the book jacket tells the reader "that nothing has been the same since Sara's father died a year ago." In Chapter 8, Sara, snuggling close to her cat Patches, says, "It's all Mom and Jon's fault. And Daddy, too. I didn't know I was mad at Daddy until the words came out of my mouth. Dads aren't supposed to go away for a weekend and never come back." Close to the conclusion of the story, Sara asks Jon, her older brother, if he thinks their dad knows what they are doing. Jon responds, "Yeah, I think so." Sara, who is frosting brownies, concurs. She says, "Me, too."

Companions Along the Way

Since early childhood, books including the journals of other writers have been my friends, companions, and teachers along the way. One of my favorite quotations is Vincent Starrett's: "When we are collecting books we are collecting happiness." As a child I read Mark Twain, Nancy Drew, Charles Dickens, myth, mystery, ghost stories, history, *Little Women, The Little Princess, The Secret Garden, Betsy and Tacy, The Canterville Ghost,* the Anne of Green Gables books, *The Wizard of Oz.*

After I began keeping my journals, I discovered other people's journals. They nourish me. May Sarton writes in *Journal of a Solitude,* "I have written novels to find out what I thought about something and poems to find out what I felt about something." Lucy Maud Montgomery's observations of nature, which she wove into the texture of her everyday experience, brought me a deeper appreciation of the natural world. Madeleine L'Engle introduced me to Montgomery's book *Emily of New Moon,* encouraged me to write, and gave me hope.

As I write, I often look up from my computer Montgomery— named after Lucy Maud Montgomery—and see the books that are waiting to be read . . . the books waiting for me to read them again. One of my favorite quotations related to reading comes from Naomi Shihab Nye: "Reading opens us up so we can live anywhere."

Quotes are also guides along the way. I have a graffiti wall and a quote-collection journal.

March 12, 1996: Reading *Deep Water Passage,* the words "Trust the journey, day by day," were the words I needed to hear, to see. A signpost along the way.

A few of my favorite quotations:

"Hope is the thing with feathers that perches on the soul."
    — Emily Dickinson
"In quietness and in confidence shall be your strength."
    — Isaiah 30:15
"What would the world do without tea? I am glad I was not
    born before tea." — Sydney Smith, 1855
"The world is but a canvas to our imagination." — Thoreau

"Story is given to you through the process of writing."
— Naomi Shihab Nye
"May the Force be with you." — Star Wars

Spiritual Reflections

December 20, 1987: Busy! Overwhelmed. God help me. How am I going to seat and feed everyone.

December 29, 1987: Christmas has come and gone. I fed thirty-one people and everyone found a place to sit. The day after Christmas, on a whim, I opened the Bible. It opened to the story of the loaves and the fishes. God definitely has a sense of humor.

February 2, 1976: The cardinal came back! He is at the feeder. I knew he was out there—somewhere—but he's out of sight until you put out the seeds. So it is with God. You sow seeds of faith and hope in cold ground. And then when you least expect it, you feel the presence and beauty of God. But first you must sow the seeds.

Safe Harbor

When asked how I would describe my journals I replied, "A safe harbor. Here I find shelter. I tie up. Think. Be. Breathe. Seek and find what I need to know."

June 10, 1997: Strange how thoughts occur. Thoughts that give you insight into the why's. The knowing that I write for that eleven, twelve, thirteen year old child who is still part of who I am. I write what that child needs to know. My writing takes me where that child needs to go. Faraway places.

My journals travel with me as I roam uncharted waters.

Jack Gantos

"Hannibal Crossing the Alps"

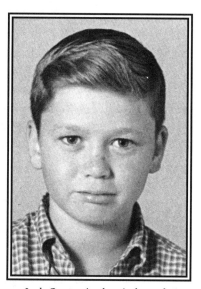

Jack Gantos in the sixth grade

Jack Gantos got hooked on the writing habit in the second grade, when his older, "smarter" sister was given a diary. He thought it was the coolest thing he had ever seen and wanted one of his own. His mother said he was too young, but relented after watching his fits and riots on the kitchen floor. With his new diary Gantos immediately discovered two things: the key did not fit the bathroom door as he had hoped (in order to get some personal and writing privacy) and he didn't have a clue what to write about.

To his sister he was "pond scum," but she shared sound literary advice. "Write what you love." Gantos loved food so he kept a menu of everything he ate. If he chewed gum, he wrote "chewed gum." He even taped in the wrapper. He had a mad crush on Carol Forbes, the girl next door, and spent a jar of pennies on her. He kept a strict accounting of how he spent each one of the seven hundred pennies. After a time he moved on from food and tackled the everyday craziness that he found in his life. He wrote stories about his family and friends and his secret inner thoughts. One day he found out that the key that wouldn't lock the bathroom door did open his sister's diary. Then he came to realize that he was the better writer.

Adolescence was a bad time for this diary keeper. Walking around school with a diary would have been an open invitation for people to make ruthless fun of him. Because he liked to write in his diary all the time, he needed it with him constantly. That's when he invented a mobile matchbox diary. Taking matchboxes from restaurants, removing the matches and sliding little slips of paper inside, Gantos made diaries small enough to fit into his pocket.

Everything made it into his diary: episodes from his anemic social life, secret crushes, descriptions of buildings and people in his new neighborhoods. In high school, Gantos says, he lost some of his zip and the blank page wasn't as stimulating. He expanded his habit of taping and pasting: stamps, bugs, movie ticket stubs, fortunes, horoscopes, postcards and photographs.

Today, Gantos needs a lot of "bang for his buck." His demanding writing and speaking schedule prevents him from sitting down and filling ten journal pages. The result: a new invention — Jack's Combo Journal. A unique blend of first-draft fiction writing and personal writing, the combo journal is a small, portable active file cabinet. For their mobility, and because he can fill a page quickly then delight in turning to a new one, Gantos uses 4-by-5-inch bound, black sketch books. Every time he begins writing a new book, he starts a new journal. He writes fiction on one page, then flips the book over to record personal "Jack life" on the opposite side. This way, he finds, his everyday life spills over into his fiction.

Gantos also carries other contrivances in his pocket: a fold-up journal that looks like a burrito filled with pages and a package of Post-it notes, a takeoff on his early matchbox journals.

Known for his *Rotten Ralph* picture books, the Jack Henry series of autobiographical stories, and creative writing presentations to teachers and students nationwide, Gantos tells kids that their journal is the single most important book they will ever write. He urges them to go after the significant, juicy things in their lives, to go out on the edge, make outrageous observations, go beyond "Dear Diary" and smiley faces. From the writer who has squished beetles, spiders, and mice skins in his journal comes this advice: When it comes to keeping a journal, anything goes.

Jack Gantos's books include

Heads or Tails: Stories from the Sixth Grade
Jack's New Power: Stories from a Caribbean Year
Jack's Black Book
Joey Pigza Swallowed the Key
Desire Lines
The *Rotten Ralph* series of picture books

The Interview

It was my sister's idea. She was two and a half years older, an adult as far as I was concerned. Compared to her I was pond scum. I was also a huge copycat. Anything my older sister did I had to do, too. Actually it was a wise choice because she was really smart. It was a way of drafting off of her great intelligence. Unfortunately, I missed all of her great grace. She got a journal, one of those year diaries with a lock and key. I thought I would lose my mind because I figured it was about the coolest thing I'd ever seen. And, I thought the key was awesome. Part of the key thing was because my mother wouldn't let me lock the bathroom door because she thought I might go in and fill up the tub and drown myself. When I saw my sister's journal with the key, the reason I wanted a journal was because I wanted the key, and the reason I wanted the key was because I thought I could lock the bathroom door. I made life very unpleasant for my mother until I got the journal and then, of course, the key didn't fit the bathroom lock.

Second-Grade Rat

I got my first journal in the second grade and it was a significant piece of private property, of great importance to me, just as important as a button is to Corduroy. Back then my journal keeping was episodic; something had to happen for me to write about it. I had an absolute mad crush on Carol Forbes. She lived next door, of course. I had a jar of pennies, seven dollars in pennies, and I spent the whole thing on Carol Forbes. I remember keeping a very strict accounting of where those pennies went. When I was getting early advice from my sister, I remember saying to her one day, "Well, what should I write about?" And she said, "Simple, write about what you love," and that was very good advice. I loved food. I was a huge eater as a child so I kept a menu of everything I ate. I'd have the journal with me, so if I chewed gum, I'd write down "chewed gum," and I'd save the wrapper and tape it in. Some of those early journals have more stuff in them than writing.

I'll tell you how I kept my sister from snooping in my journal. I was riding my bike down the street one day and I saw a road-kill mouse. I scraped it up and put it in the front of my journal. So I had a scab-like flattened mouse on the title page. That protected my journal. Of course, I was snooping in hers because I found out those little keys fit every journal on the planet. I would go into her bedroom, open her drawer, take it out, unlock it, and copy entire passages from my sister's journal into mine. It was the moment I realized I could write better than my sister.

Jack's Wart Relic

Adolescence was a bad time. In adolescence the journal writing waned, largely because we never had journal writing in school. I never called my journal a journal. I called it a diary. When I grew up, the gender of the word diary was definitely female. Guys did not keep diaries. So, it was really hard for me to walk around school with a diary. I might as well have just asked for people to come up and make ruthless fun of me. The diary did not become mobile. I kept it at home. It was almost embarrassing to write in it because I felt like I was doing a girl thing. I never knew any guys who wrote or met any writers. I wanted to write, but there was no example in the universe as far as I knew of a guy doing what I was doing. That's when I started making the matchbox journals. I would take matches from restaurants, pull out the drawer, throw out the matches, and cut slips of paper to fit into the matchbox. When I had an idea that I didn't want to lose, I would open my matchbox and write it down. They were small, and I could keep them in my pocket and they looked like matches, which was cool, which looked like possibly, after school, you could go behind a bush and smoke a cigarette. Going behind a bush and writing in your diary was not cool.

Adolescence was a time of friendships. One thing that was predominant in those diaries was the social life—people you knew, people you wanted to know, secret crushes. I had absolutely no spine. I was really a gutless kid. When it came to being around girls, I couldn't even talk to girls. Everything would make it into the journal.

I grew up all over the place. I was born in western Pennsylvania, then moved to Cape Hatteras, then back to Pennsylvania, then to Barbados, then Miami, Fort Lauderdale, Pompano. I went to nine different schools in twelve grades. I wrote a lot about my neighborhoods, because I always found them fascinating. The people were really interesting. I liked architecture because my dad was in construction. I liked buildings and always looked keenly at them. Some people say people look like their dogs. But I think people look like their houses. I had read *Harriet the Spy,* a landmark book for me because it gave me the idea that I was allowed and sanctioned to write about people in ways that they would not necessarily like if they read it. There was something delicious about that.

In junior high I still had some zip in me, but high school was more fallow. If a journal had a pop top on it, that would have been my favorite journal. You know, a beer can shaped as a journal. We never had any creative writing. None. So the journal was a thing you did as a hobby around the house. What kept my journal alive was that I didn't always write in them, I saved stuff. My stamp collection would be in my journal, bug collection, movie ticket stub collection, Chinese fortune cookie fortunes, horoscopes, photographs, postcards, all that stuff would go in my journal. I found that if I kept stuff in the journal I would always find something to write about. That helped me a lot. That blank page in the journal was not very stimulating for me. I needed something physical to describe, attack, or inspire me in some way. Really disgusting things, too. Once I took a pair of needle-nosed pliers and I pulled a wart out of my foot. I cut a little hole in my journal and put the wart in there and put a little Scotch tape over it. It's still there, dried up.

Down and Out

When I was really poor and lived in a rooming house—ten years I lived in a rooming house on Marlborough Street in Boston—and taught at Emerson College, I had a marvelous life. I didn't publish a lot, but I kept fabulous journals—pages and pages of journals. Having that limitless time, being single, hours and hours of my own time, nobody bugging me, that's all I would do. I kept great diaries. I'd take a trip to Brazil for two months and Honduras, Nicaragua, Mexico and come back with volumes of journals, great books, that every now and again I take out and read.

Combo Journals

I don't have time now to sit down and write ten pages in my journal. Perhaps that's why I get more bang for my buck and why I have a fusion of personal writing and fiction writing between the covers. Part of the importance of journal writing is recording my thoughts, what took place: I'm pulled over by the cops, I got a ticket; I write that in. I ate something great for dinner; I write that in. I drank a good bottle of wine; I write that in. I have dreams; I put those in. It's a habit that causes me to pay attention to the immediate surface of my life. Writing about my life is prewriting for fiction writing. It spills over and I take it from there.

These days my journals are combo journals; each journal is a combination of writing for a specific book and writing about my life simultaneously. This probably sounds old fashioned, but I

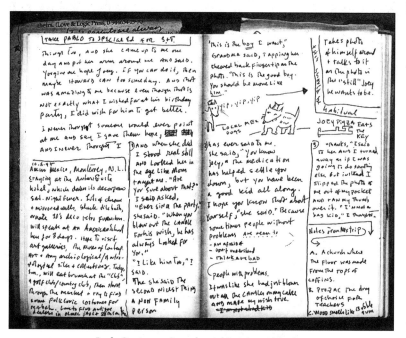

Jack Gantos writes about his trip to Mexico

like writing out everything by longhand and then typing it into my computer. When I get up in the morning and get started writing, generally I'll turn on my computer and read what I typed in the day before. But my journal is on the desk and I start writing something fresh in it. I get a rough draft in the journal and then type it into the computer and then work on that. My journals end up being rough and ready. Rough, really, really rough versions of the novel. Years ago, before the computer, I would write the second draft longhand in my journal.

Every time I start a new book, I start a new journal. Sometimes what I do is write the fiction on one side of the journal, like a regular book, starting in, then I flip it over so it's upside down and I work that way on the personal life. I buy 4-by-5-inch bound black sketchbooks at the art supply store. They're mobile and they frequently go with me. I like small pages. I have small handwriting. I can fill up a page quickly, then delight of all delight, I get to turn the page. In those big journals you write like a fiend and you're still on the same page. That's discouraging.

I also have tabs I put in my journal to segment it. For a writer's journal I have a tab for characters, plot, vocabulary, similes, and then other tabs, too, for personal Jack life. It's like an active file cabinet of themes, characters, stories, and novel proposals, speculations, possibilities. I like to see how it adds up together and I like reading through it to see the resonance between the life and writing, and there generally are some pretty telling correspondences.

A lot of times my journals remain alive for the next book. For example, in the Jack books—*Heads or Tails, Jack's New Power, Jack's Black Book*—since it's all the same character the journals carry over to the next book. Even as I was writing *Heads or Tails* I would think of a story and decide that it's not going to fit into this book, so I'd then tab a section for future stories. The journal has to stay alive because I have material in there that's planted that I don't want to lose.

Grown-up Imaginary Friend

As an unresolved human being I've got journals where I write about the stubbed toe of life. Many of my journals are filled with the driveling of a driveler to a grown-up version of an imaginary friend. Imaginary friends are good. Kids learn a lot from them. They learn empathy and they learn how to see something from another point of view, which is key if they're going to be real human beings. When I look at my personal life over the years, whenever I'm down and out . . kicked around like a dog . . . broken-hearted . . . girlfriend left . . . man, can I fill a journal. That journal was warm all the time from having my hand on it. There's a lot of stream-of-consciousness stuff, which is really good for when I'm out there howling at the moon with a thorn in my paw. When things are hopping good—I wake up, my wife and I are still in love, life is good—I don't write it down as often.

A Writer's Journal

Keeping a journal is the first thing I talk to kids about. I show them my journals, show them several. I tell them this is the single most important book that they will write. Whether they become poets or novelists, or better business letter writers, that's fine. I hope they do. At the end of their lives the books they are going to be most satisfied with are their journals. It's a good writing habit, and it's a way to discover important truths about yourself, truths you can transfer to the lives of your characters.

I get at them to go after the subjects that are the most significant, juicy things in their lives. The things that are seemingly taboo, the deepest feelings, the most outrageous observations, things that when they think it, they think, "Am I going to get in trouble for this?"

I'm asking them to go out on the edge and be as honest and forthright as they possibly can be because that is where they will discover who they are and they will discover a language for articulating who they are and what they see.

I always tell teachers to write responses on Post-it notes, because kids don't want red ink in their journals. I talk to them about the two different kinds of journals, the story journal and the personal journal. Maybe the personal journal isn't monitored and the story journal is. I want to get beyond the "dear diary"—the dear diary is the padded diary, with smiley faces—I'm talking about a writer's journal where you sit down and say to yourself what interesting stuff did I see today? What did I hear? What am I thinking about that is interesting to me? How do I fit it into a story?

Hannibal Crossing the Alps

When you write about yourself, observations, activities, speculations against those activities, and other people's lives, you're expanding who you are, stretching the boundaries of who you are, and you're becoming an ever-larger person. You're expanding your territories. You're Hannibal crossing the Alps. It gives you more range as a human being to look at people and speculate into their lives, look at locations and imagine what situations could take place within those locations. You do that in your journal. You do that freely. You do that without thinking, "Where is this going, how does it fit my plot?" You are on free time, anything goes. It's a free-for-all, it's a romp. You're always surprised by what you write and that's part of the great joy of it.

No Lost Journals

I don't have any lost diary stories. Of my two hundred volumes, I've never lost any. It would set me back years. I always put my address and phone number on the inside of my journal and I put down Reward Offered. I'm thinking of taping a $20 bill on the inside with a note: "Here's twenty bucks, this is just the beginning of the reward." You lose these things and it's like your house burning down.

When I lived in the rooming house, I read somewhere that if your house burns down, the only things that would stay intact is what's in the refrigerator. So I used to keep all my manuscripts and journals in the refrigerator lined up on those steel racks like bookshelves. A library on ice. You could buy an extra refrigerator or you could do what people do: you could buy a safe.

Once I was on the Amazon, actually the Rio Negro—the Amazon is actually made up of lots of rivers—and I was where the Rio Negro meets up with the Rio Solomon on the west side of Manaus. I was in a dugout canoe by myself out there paddling around. I always would keep my camera and my journal and important things in a zip-lock bag. God forbid, if I would tip over, it would float. The reason I tipped over is because a giant spider monkey jumps in my canoe and he's coming at me and I don't know what to do. Is this like man meets beast or is this the peaceable kingdom or is this like Darwin and this thing is going to take a bite out of me?

The other thing about the Rio Negro is that it is filled with piranhas. The piranhas aren't going to bother you, said my handbook, unless you're already bleeding. Of course, you're never sure of this rather odd information. It could have been a Brazilian old wive's tale, but I didn't want to test it out. Still, the monkey advanced, the canoe rocks and we tip. When I surface I'm thinking I've got a monkey guarding the upside-down canoe, I've got piranhas under me, and I've got my diary in a zip-lock bag floating down the Amazon. What to do first? Definitely get the diary.

Mary E. Lyons

"From Heart to Head to Hand"

Mary E. Lyons, age 6

Honoring her subjects' spirits is essential for biographer and historical fiction author Mary E. Lyons. To bridge time spans and cultural chasms, Lyons travels to her subjects' hometowns, visits family homesteads, cradles objects they once held in their hands. In libraries, archives, and museums she searches for evidence. To hear their voices, discern their vulnerabilities, and merge with her characters' personalities, Lyons converses with them on the pages of her journal.

When she was fifteen, Lyons spent a nine-month period as a diary keeper. From December 28, 1961, to September 26, 1962, she recorded the weather and notes about boys, clothes, moods, and her mercurial emotions. She underlined, capitalized, and emphasized with exclamation points. Lyons can't explain why she set aside her diary. Perhaps, she thinks, the burgundy leatherette cover, which was the same color as her horrible-tasting cough medicine, repulsed her. Thirty years later, when she began writing *Keeping Secrets*, her study of the adolescent diaries of seven women writers, Lyons reread the burgundy leatherette diary. She cried as she reentered her world of coming-of-age frustrations, jealousies, and excitements. Lyons connected with her subjects' young spirits and voices to evoke nineteenth-century personalities who often lived out their emotional lives between the covers of secret diaries.

As she delved into the private lives of Louisa May Alcott, Charlotte Forten, Sarah Jane Foster, Kate Chopin, Alice Dunbar-Nelson, Ida B. Wells, and Charlotte Perkins Gilman, Lyons herself returned to keeping a personal diary. Always afraid this diary would be discovered, she hid it away, well aware that her husband, the only other person living in the house, wouldn't peek. She even instructed a friend to destroy her journal in case of emergency. Only when she was alone in the empty house could she manage to write diary entries. At first, committing confidences to the page was tortuous; the process, she found, was "formal, tentative, like a conversation with a stranger on a bus." Later, it became familiar and easy—words flowing "from heart to head to hand." While researching and writing *Keeping Secrets*, Lyons used her parallel diary to think through problems encountered writing the book, to record conversations with her editor and to probe her emotional life. Because of the honesty she was finally able to tap, Lyons vows it is the only diary she will ever destroy.

When Lyons finished *Keeping Secrets*, she explored other forms of journal keeping, always trying to make connections to her subject's spirit. Now, several writer's notebooks accompany each book she writes: research notes, rough outlines, thoughts quickly written down, newspaper files covered with her scribbling. In a separate journal, entitled "Words and Phrases," she stores bits of overheard conversations and descriptive lines that pop into her mind.

Early in the conception of *Letters From A Slave Girl*, her first work of historical fiction, Lyons sat down with a yellow legal pad on her lap. Morning light slanted in through her living room window. The house was empty and still. Without planning to, she began devising a list of all the ways she identified with her protagonist Harriet Jacobs—when both were twelve years old. Lyons describes this journal-writing moment as pivotal to capturing the voice she was trying to create.

As she writes, her characters speak to her. To get to know him better, Lyons set a place at the dinner table for Moses Williams of *The Poison Place*. Then she purchased a book where she could record what he was telling her. On the inside of the book she filled in his name: "This book belongs to Moses Williams." Lyons discovered that keeping a fictional diary allowed her to enter deeply into Moses' character.

"Often I think about my subject's feelings so much," writes Lyons, "I begin to think we are the same person." On the pages of her journals, words from her heart and head mingle with those of her subjects and characters. As Lyons breathes life into their spirits, her words flow freely from her hand and into the hearts of adolescent readers.

Mary E. Lyons's books include

Sorrow's Kitchen: The Life and Folklore of Zora Neal Hurston
Letters from a Slave Girl: The Story of Harriet Jacobs
Catching the Fire: Philip Simmons, Blacksmith
Keeping Secrets: The Girlhood Diaries of Seven Women Writers
The Poison Place
Talking with Tebé: Clementine Hunter, Memory Artist (editor)

The Interview

Tuesday, January 23, 1962: Weather record: cloudy
Wore plaid purple skirt and sweater. Went to Marilyn's after
school and copied Shakespeare's life from her encyclopedia. She
gave me a whole package of old notes. HILARIOUS! The things we
write about! Sex, G.M., boys, gossip about new girls, ANYTHING!
Didn't see Eberhart. Patrick has the flu. He was fussy all afternoon, has diaraeha [sic] and fever.

I kept a girlhood diary from December 28, 1961 to September
26, 1962. I can't say why I got started . . . maybe it was a
Christmas present. There was a one-inch box on each page for
the weather, which I always filled in. The diary was ugly—burgundy leatherette. It was the same color as the cough medicine
I once took for the flu. The medicine made me throw up, and I
think that's why I eventually quit writing in the diary . . . every
time I looked at it I felt sick.

When I began writing *Keeping Secrets: The Girlhood Diaries of
Seven Women Writers,* I dug out that old diary. Rereading it
made me cry. Not only because of the toe problems I had as a
fifteen-year-old—and I had a lot of toe problems! When I identified threads from 1962 that have carried over to my adult life—
feelings of alienation, not fitting in—they startled me. I didn't
realize the significance of those feelings at the time, but here
they are, part of my adult identity. My 1962 diary helped me see
fissures that opened so long ago, and I wept to realize how early
on in life this pain begins. But the diary also helped me identify similar threads in the lives of the women I was researching.
Threads that began in girlhood remained throughout their lives.

Parallel Journeys, Parallel Journals

Keeping Secrets was the first book I wrote after I began writing full time. It was a period of great transition for me because
I had left a secure job in a school system to go off on my own.

Since I was delving into the private thoughts of seven women during their greatest times of transition, it seemed only fair to keep a private record of my life, too. While I have kept different kinds of journals sporadically all my life, I never considered myself a traditional diary keeper. This time I decided to be very deliberate in my diary keeping during the writing of this book.

In *Keeping Secrets,* I focused on the girlhood journal entries of Louisa May Alcott, Charlotte Forten, Sarah Jane Foster, Kate Chopin, Alice Dunbar Nelson, Ida B. Wells, and Charlotte Perkins. Feminist scholars have concentrated on these women as writers and literary figures. Often scholars start at a point at which the women are grown up.

But it was these younger voices that captivated me. The young women's diaries are filled with emotion—underlining, capitalization, and a plethora of exclamation points. I found all those things in my 1962 diary, too. The frustrations with parents, jealousy, depression, or excitement we feel at fifteen, we feel for the rest of our lives, even though we might not access these feelings so easily as adults.

As I wrote *Keeping Secrets,* I reread my early diary. I identified with these women as girls and I went back to that younger part of myself, painful as it was. I even decided to get braces in the middle of writing the book.

February 22, 1994
My mother's advice was always full of potholes. She said, "Tell me everything," then refused to listen. "Be yourself," she counseled, then let me know the many ways I disappointed. "I always wanted a little girl with blue eyes and curly black hair," she said dreamily, in front of the little girl with hazel eyes and straight hair. "I always wore the prettiest clothes. Everything matched," she said to the girl who washed out the same pair of socks each night.

"Nothing in this life is perfect. The hardest thing in life is getting along with other people." These were the guidelines I received, while other girls got piano lessons and braces and new Easter dresses and manners with which to find their way.

Keeping My Secrets

Because it looked as feminine as nineteenth-century diaries, I decided to use a spiral memo pad with purple pansies on the cover. It took me a while to get comfortable with being honest. I say in an early entry, "I'm fascinated by the diaries of these women and what they've written or hidden between the lines— a voyeuristic pleasure. But I find it difficult to be precisely honest here in my own writing partly because I'm so afraid it will be found." Later I reflect on this entry. "Thoughts on the diary process: formal, tentative, like a conversation with a stranger on a bus. Now it's a more familiar process. The words take a direct process from heart to head to hand."

I still keep this diary hidden away. My husband is here, and though I know he won't read it, there's a chance that another human being might see it. I had to have an operation halfway through writing the book. On the way to the hospital at 6 A.M. I saw a friend. I stopped her and said, "Look, I have this diary and I'm going to tell you exactly where it is. If something happens to me, go get it. Destroy it." It's the only diary I will get rid of. I don't know when, but I am sure I will throw it away.

11/14/93

Such a week . . . NY on Tuesday to accept award. "I speak fine," as Alice Dunbar-Nelson said in her diary. Lunch with M. Once the editorial surgery started, his tiny office seemed frightful and familiar— it could have been any principal, doctor, lawyer, priest sitting there. Omniscient in manner, authoritative in tone, he was a Man in Charge of the Little Woman. I fought back the tears. He had a job to do, but he went too far. "That's the way we do it here," he said.

Maybe I can't write this book. When I am through with this diary, I will boil it. Hard white words will be left on the bottom of the pot. I'll put them in a box and shake them every now and then to remember.

Writing Notebooks

(From Lyons's Letters From a Slave Girl diary)

When in garret she sometimes thinks that God is a mystery since he allowed slavery & a man like Vorcom. She is angry with Him, perhaps even doubting his existence. I believe that after Harriet discussed her situation (sexual choice—babies) with her daughter, that the healing process began. Just as Eileen's healthy attitude toward sex provided a sort of "approval by proxy" from Mom, so did Louisa become a mother (grandmother) figure for Harriet. And who better than the very illegitimate child—the one who had to wear the label that Harriet must have felt responsible for.

I keep several notebooks going for each book I write—chronologies, articles I've hole-punched, research notes, rough outlines, my thoughts quickly written down. It is important that I do the scribbling stage, the planning and outlining, by hand. When I was writing *The Poison Place,* the characters started talking to me. I decided to buy a little book where I could record what they were saying. I went to a stationery store and deliberated over a display of blank books. It was extremely important that it look just right. One journal had a reproduction of a painting by Raphael on the cover. Since there is a character named Raphaelle in the *The Poison Place,* I chose this for my idea book. I have a terrible memory and don't trust myself to remember phrases that come to me. I knew this was the only way the voices wouldn't get lost in the voluminous notes I took while researching *The Poison Place.*

The character who tells the story of *The Poison Place* speaks in first-person dramatic monologue. His name is Moses Williams. Moses is black and Raphaelle is white, and the book is about their friendship. On the inside of the blank book I filled in the line "This book belongs to ____" with the name Moses Williams. I began keeping a journal for a fictional character. Pretending it was his diary helped me enter more deeply into his character.

Journal Writing Moments

Journal writing is a kind of meditation, a way of being still and listening. I do it as needed and always alone. I couldn't possibly write with anyone else in the room. Preferably no one else is in the house. When I was writing *Letters From a Slave Girl,* my first work of historical fiction, I woke up very early one morning and went down to the living room. I sat with a legal pad, making a list of all the ways that I identified with Harriet Jacobs when she and I were twelve. This was nothing that I had planned. It was a journal writing moment that turned out to be pivotal for the voice I was about to create.

In Their Own Words

By reading the girlhood journals of the seven women writers I discussed in *Keeping Secrets,* I connected with the lives and literature. It's one thing to read what has been written about a woman, but one has such a different feeling after reading journal entries in which vulnerability and emotion are expressed. The journals reminded me that women's concerns are universal. Because I was better able to understand these concerns by reading diaries, I was better able to understand myself. My advice to young people: If you don't want to write your own journal, then read published diaries by someone else. They have much to teach us.

> 2/18/93
> After reading that [1962] diary last Sunday, I was inconsolable all day—all those problems still hanging around my neck. This is what I need to put in the introduction [to *Keeping Secrets*]. That we think we're so flawed, but the diary can show us a way out if we listen to ourselves. That each of us is a grand mix. Honor the bad feelings—soothe, accept, explore. Celebrate the good.

Marion Dane Bauer

"Half-Guilty Hobby"

Marion Dane Bauer as a teenager

Growing up in a family where it wasn't considered polite to acknowledge, talk about, or worse yet, display emotions, Marion Dane Bauer often got herself into trouble. Her scientist father leaned on logic; her mother remained silent. Even her brother sided with their father's insistence on restraint and rationality. Out of step with her family's emotional rigidity, Bauer retreated to her bedroom or sought refuge in the surrounding woods. Confused and hurt and left alone with her spirited imagination and a head spinning with stories, Bauer instinctively turned inward. Before long, she came to value her imagination, privacy, and deep emotional responses to life.

"I think most children's writers were, for one reason or another, lonely children," she says. "And that loneliness, while it certainly had its negative side, was, for each of us, an occasion for developing rich inner resources."

Time alone offered more hours for reading and creating stories of her own. Friends were available, but not on the daily basis Bauer might have liked. At age seven, when she moved with her family into a large home close to the cement mill where her father worked as a chemical engineer, Bauer was closer to the daughters of the mill superintendent. But they attended a different school. While she had friends at church and at dance school, Bauer lived in a neighborhood where boys vastly outnumbered the girls. If a playmate were available, Bauer wrote stories for both of them to act out, always careful that the rising tension of the plot be resolved happily to keep her playmate coming back. Playing by herself, using dolls, hollyhock blooms, or marbles for people, Bauer dramatized stories and directed all the action, adventures, and arguments.

When Bauer began writing fiction for children, she drew on her experiences of childhood and discovered in those forbidden feelings a rich trove of stories. According to Bauer, satisfying the unfulfilled core of a child's longing, or "child hole," is what all fiction is about. Writing to resolve the fundamental issues of her own childhood, Bauer revisits again and again the fictional quest of an alienated child reaching out to connect with a parent or parent figure. It's her strongest theme, the one she admits she draws on consciously and continually. "I spent my childhood longing for overt approval, if not from [my parents] then from some other adult," she writes in *A Writer's Story: From Life to Fiction.*

Bauer admits that by its very nature, the child hole will never be entirely filled, "however long our therapy, however many stories we write." The need to try is the energy that sets her stories in motion. When she was in high school, this same energy propelled her to begin a correspondence with a favorite cousin. At last, she had found the safe someone with whom she could talk. Letter writing became her way to connect the inner terrain of forbidden feelings to the outer world. Letters were more than a means of communication—they were the laboratory where Bauer disciplined herself to observe the world carefully and to teach herself to write. Slipping pieces of carbon paper behind the letters, she saved copies and started her own form of journal keeping.

Paralleling her strongest literary theme, that of a child's need for connection, Bauer began writing letters to master storyteller Madeleine L'Engle in 1973, three years before her first book *Shelter from the Wind* was published. She knew no other writers and had yet to have any validation for her own career. The wife of an Episcopal bishop had sent Bauer a copy of L'Engle's *A Circle of Quiet*. Reading such a personal work was like meeting another children's writer. Afterward, Bauer went on to read L'Engle's novels. Then she sat down to write to the author. And Madeleine faithfully replied. What followed was a correspondence that lasted many years and covered professional and personal concerns and issues of faith.

Bauer came to writing with a strong need to explore feelings and legitimize them. Letter writing to trusted cousins and friends, then keeping a personal journal, helped her understand and come to terms with all that her childhood training had kept from view. Far from ignoring the childhood voice that still cries, "Pay attention to me," Bauer feels privileged to write from that place of unfulfilled longing, one formed in her lonely childhood. In the creative isolation of the writer's life, Bauer felt fortunate to have Madeleine L'Engle. As her own career has matured, being a mentor is a responsibility Bauer has come to take seriously. Serving as faculty chair of Vermont College's Master of Fine Arts in Writing for Children, teaching writing workshops, and critiquing manuscripts are just a few of the many ways Newbery Honor author Marion Dane Bauer helps developing writers find their own stories and sharpen their literary skills.

Marion Dane Bauer's books include

What's Your Story: A Young Person's Guide to Writing Fiction
A Writer's Story: From Life to Fiction
On My Honor
Bear's Hiccups
If You Were Born a Kitten
A Taste of Smoke

The Interview

I didn't begin anything that faintly resembled a journal until I had learned to type at the age of thirteen. If you'd ask me what I'd wanted to be when I was a child I would have said a poet, not a writer. It wasn't because I loved poems more than stories—I always loved stories—but because I perceived poems as being short and stories as being long. Writing by hand has always been very tedious for me. It's not something I'm comfortable with, though I have wondered sometimes if a different, less polished, less audience-oriented kind of writing might happen by hand. And I suppose it does, but the writing feels limiting because there's so much I don't say because I don't want to bother to have to write it down.

My earliest journal entries were letters. When I was in high school, after I'd learned to type, I began writing long letters to a favorite cousin. Early on I began the process of slipping a piece of carbon paper and a second sheet into the typewriter. I kept those copies of the letters. What I was doing was writing to someone with whom I felt safe, someone who I felt did care about what I was putting on paper. Over the years my cousin evolved into other people who became important to me. It was from the letter writing that I then began writing for myself, in a journal, though very often there was one other person, a close friend, with whom I shared my journals.

Emotions into Words

My journal was a friend, a place to go with feelings that weren't safe to express in my life, that would have been dismissed or criticized or offensive to other people in some way. I wrote in my journal when the occasion either offered itself or demanded it in an emotional way. It would depend on what was going on in my life and how much need I had to understand it. I grew up in a family where feelings weren't considered quite nice and I had to have some place to go with them. For years my journal was a safe place to go when things were painful or confusing or just very private. In it I learned to process my feelings and I learned to find language for the world around me.

Writing was such a constant process that I never had a problem with privacy. Nobody in the family was the least bit interested in what I was putting on paper. I always figured that I was totally safe because it wouldn't have occurred to anybody even to pick up a piece of paper that I had put something on.

Writing to Be Shared

Most of the time journal keeping was not a very private thing. I needed there to be an audience, in exactly the same way that I need an audience for my fiction, though the audience I desired was much more limited. I needed one other person in my life with whom I would be sharing.

I can remember when I was teaching high school. On Saturday mornings when my former husband was then in seminary and when all the other working seminary wives were dutifully cleaning their one-room apartments, I was journaling. About noon I would be done and I would go down to visit my friend, the one who would read my journals, and her apartment was just sparkling. I would have a hunk of journal in my hand, and she would dutifully sit down and read it.

On the one hand journaling was always a kind of half-guilty

```
                          July 24, 1979
     Dear Madeleine,

          I have spent most of the day reading various of Katherine
     Ann Porter's novels, some for the first time--except for the
     afternoon spent reading something for one of my former students--
     and I am feeling nearly mesmerized.  I picked up a book of her
     short stories, ready to head for bed with it, but on my way to bed
     I got enough incontrol of my brain to divert myself to the type-
     writer to write to you.  There comes a point when the brain quits
     absorbing.  Tomorrow I will clean out the refrigerator and go have
     lunch with a friend I don't see often enough because I don't put my
     work down to take the time.  Maybe that will give the brain tissue
     time to reconstitute itself.

          I finished the third draft on TANGLED BUTTERFLY in the first
     days of July.  I expect to hear from Jim in early August, time
     enough left for dealing with minor problems.  If there is much
     left that isn't minor, we will have to set a new deadline.  I
     think, though, that it's done.  I wish it were possible, at the
     end of the work, to resurrect more of the excitement and
     confidence that went into the story's planning back at the begin-
     ning.  Everything seems so pure in the planning, so certain to be
     the best, to be finally the tale I have always meant to tell.
     When it is done, there is pride in it, satisfaction, a willingness
     to let go similar to releasing the ties on a child, but through
     all of it, something of a sense of having failed.  I didnnot, then,
     create that perfect novel that seemed to be promised in its con-
     ception.  I didn't even come close.  Oh well...on to the next one.
     This one, of course, will be different.

          Of course, these are patterns I am just beginning to dis-
     tinguish, just beginning to have been around the process long
     enough to see that patterns exist.  If they are universal and
     not just personal--as I assume they are--you will have been through
     them many times.  A much beloved cousin was here, six years older
     than I, a very important figure in my growing up years.  She and I
     hadn't seen one another for over twenty years.  I was talking to
     her about the feeling I find myself with, that of wanting to draw
     in all the edges of my work, to simplify, to find some core within
     myself and to stay there.  I've been at this work now--really at it--
     for seven years.  (That must seem a short time to you.)  In the
     first five it was my deepest, best play.  I woke up every morning
     and was thrilled that I would be permitted to do it.  It is sur-
     prising now that I look back that such a period could have lasted
     for five years.  In the time since then, it has become my work.
     Good work.  Solid work.  There is none other I could think of doing.
     And some days, when I discover some small important piece about
     what I am doing, the old excitment rages briefly, but mostly I do
     it because I choose to do it, because it is difficult to imagine
     doing anything else.  And I come to the end of a piece and I wish
     that I were more, that my craft were deeper so that I could come
     closer to something I have only dreamed.  She, the cousin whom I
     have left far behind in this paragraph, said, "Don't you realize
     tha
```

From a letter to Madeleine L'Engle

hobby. In those early years it was always a matter of taking time away from "more important things" like cleaning the house. The pleasure came partly from the connection it gave me with the person I shared it with, both when I was writing letters and when I was sharing my journal.

Journal as Writing Laboratory

I taught myself to write by keeping a journal. In those early years I would create stories out of those little events that had happened to me and turn something rather mundane into a good story along the way. I was a very honest person until I sat down to write. The raw material really was never quite good enough to suit my purposes.

I don't go back and reread my journals. Once I've written something down, it's plugged into my brain, and even though I wouldn't do it in exactly the same words again, the next time I hit the same topic I have the facility of having already been through it. I'll write it again with more ease and probably with more grace than I had the first time.

Though I'm sure there are things that I could go back and pull out, there's something about going back to who I was and where I was and what I was struggling with at the time that I find very disheartening. I just don't want to look at it that closely. What's valuable is that I've written it. It's more imprinted than it would have been otherwise.

Journal writing helps writers because it keeps the writing muscles limber, the muscles of the brain flexible, and it develops facility with language just by the fact that day after day one is searching for the right word and the right phrase and feeling the flow of writing. Journal keepers come to know themselves, and through knowing themselves they will come to understand other people. It's certainly this understanding that lies at the basis of most creative writing.

Letting Go

A few years ago I made a shift when I began attempting some journaling by hand. I began to need to separate my work, which was at a keyboard, from journaling. I had a bound book and did some journaling by hand that was connected with meditating in the morning. I also read spiritual readings, then meditated, then journaled. I'm not sure how long that lasted, maybe a year or two, not steadily, not every day, but off and on, and that has fallen away.

I haven't kept a journal now for the past few years. When I began walking in the morning instead of sitting and meditating, journal writing didn't fit. I have found it difficult in recent years to do what I would call recreational writing or personal writing. It is hard to use my work time for journal writing.

Journal Legacy

I haven't thought about what will happen to my journals, or if I have it's been one of those things that flips through my mind and I push it right out. My daughter is set up to be my literary executor. Or my partner would be if she survives me. My own instinct is that nobody's going to care enough about them to do much of anything with them. I think they will probably get tossed along the way and that's fine. I'm just not going to be the one to toss them. I can't imagine my family wading through them. I really cannot, though families always surprise us. Maybe there will be a grandchild who from that distance will have more of a passionate interest.

My children grew up with mother writing, and while they certainly read my books and responded to my books there was never any urgency on their part about seeing what I was putting on paper. So I can't imagine them wanting to wade through these journals.

Literary Companions

Occasionally I pick up a published journal. I probably need to try that more, because in the last few years I've become rather impatient with much of the fiction I'm reading. I need to find some kinds of nonfiction writing that serve my needs. Journal writing may be one of those, but I just haven't explored it very deeply. I read almost exclusively contemporary fiction, both adults' and children's. Story used to be to me a kind of salvation. Story was what was going to fix the world. If I can find a novel that just sets me on my ear for the beauty of its language and the penetration of its characters and the depth of its insight, I love it. It's still just thrilling, but I find it harder and harder to find those pieces that do that for me and I find myself more and more impatient with the ones that don't do it.

Recording the Inner Life

One of the main things I say to children is don't turn journal writing into an obligation, don't start recording what you did, what you ate, and what you wore, but make it more spontaneous and more of a record of your inner life, of what's important to you. Write what you're feeling, when you're angry, when you're happy, when you've made a discovery.

For children keeping journals in classrooms, one of two things needs to happen. Either it needs to be very clear that this is a journal for an audience, therefore what they're writing they need to feel safe sharing. Or there needs to be an arrangement with the teacher where the teacher will read only what he or she has permission to read. And then, of course, the teacher must earn the child's trust.

Pam Conrad

"Time Capsule"

Pam Conrad, summer 1995

As a child, Pam Conrad followed her mother's example and recorded her life in the diaries she received every year for Christmas. When Conrad married, her mother surprised her with a special wedding gift: her own diaries typed up to be presented to her daughter. "I have a record of my whole childhood, from the time I was in second grade and we moved into our house until I got married," she said.

Conrad loved leafing back through her mother's journals to remember her life as a little girl, even if the stories were told from her mother's point of view. Conrad, who saw little direct connection between her life as a writer and her life as a journal keeper, knew she would have carried on the family tradition of writing in a journal, even if she hadn't become a writer.

Writing in her journal in an increasingly authentic voice evolved gradually for Conrad as she matured. During her young married years, she said, she felt compelled to present a Pollyanna picture of her life. "It was hard for me to admit that maybe things weren't one hundred percent. I always made it sound like life was wonderful." Later she was able to capture life's events in all their complexities. Ultimately, Conrad realized that she wrote in her journal primarily to create a "time capsule" of her past.

Conrad's interest in history and in journal writing inspired her to create an account of Christopher Columbus's voyage in journal format. In her author's note to *Pedro's Journal: A Voyage with Christopher Columbus August 3, 1492—February 14, 1493*, Conrad explains her purpose: "to sail through a brief period of history inside the heart and mind of a young boy, one Pedro de Salcedo." Taken along aboard the Santa Maria with Captain Columbus, Pedro assumes favored status as ship's boy because he can read and write. In his journal, Pedro captures the drama of the voyage and discusses his journal-keeping habits. Sometimes life is too hectic and once he thinks of censoring material his mother might find offensive.

> October 16: After seeing "beautiful, strong, naked people," Pedro confides in his journal: "There is so much to remember and record, and so much I do not think I want to tell my mother. Perhaps I will keep these letters to myself."

> December 13: "It is difficult to keep a journal now that we are so busy traveling from island to island, up and down rivers and in and out of harbors."

> December 25: After Pedro loses status as favored ship's boy the night the Santa Maria hits a barrier reef with him at helm, he tells his journal, "I am lucky to still have my journal."

> February 14: Now aboard the Nina in stormy seas on the return voyage, Pedro complains: "Everything is drenched with salt water

except this journal and the Captain's log, which we keep wrapped together high on a shuttered shelf."

Certain the Nina will go down, Columbus finishes his account of the voyage and his discoveries and tells Pedro, "We will wrap my proclamation in a waxed cloth, seal it in a wooden barrel, and cast it into the sea. If we don't return, may the truth return without us." Columbus offers to include Pedro's journal.

Pedro agrees: "I hold you in my hands. You are still dry, so Go with God. Tell God where I am."

Here Pedro's journal ends, but the story does not. The Nina stays afloat, and Pedro returns to his mother. Somewhere in the Atlantic Ocean, Pedro's journal, a time capsule of the past, remains safe and dry until it is discovered nearly five hundred years after the voyage. Pedro's loving attempts to provide both for his journal's safety and for its posterity echo matters dear to Pam Conrad's heart.

Whether it was writing by hand in a cloth-bound journal following morning meditation on the terrace or at the computer keeping track of her professional life—conversations with editors, worries about finishing a project—Conrad wrote for herself. Once, however, Pam Conrad wrote a journal with an audience in mind.

For a few months before her daughter Sarah went off to college, Conrad kept a journal of their life together. Following a family tradition, Conrad surprised her daughter with this journal, the precious account of what their lives were like while they still had time together.

Pam Conrad died in 1996, shortly after this interview.

Pam Conrad's books include

Prairie Songs
Taking the Ferry Home
My Daniel
Pedro's Journal: A Voyage with Christopher Columbus
Our House: Stories of Levittown
The Tub People

The Interview

When I was little, every year for Christmas I received a diary. I don't have those; they got lost along the way, but they were special and I remember writing in them. While I've had different kind of diaries, I usually buy a cloth-covered blank book. Every once in a while if I find something that's really unusual, that's a different size, or a little odd, I'll get it, especially if I like the paper in it.

I'm not someone who lives in her journal. I don't keep it in my pocketbook. I don't write every thought in it, although I admire people who do that. I write in my diary once a day to give me an overview of my day. It's not literature, it's not even a creative outlet. I write in my diary to remember what my life was like.

I usually meditate every morning; I do TM. So I'll meditate and if it's a nice day I'll sit out on my terrace, off of my bedroom, and write out there. Even if I hadn't been a writer I still would have kept a journal. I find I don't get creative in it, although every now and then a phrase might pop up and I'll jot it in my journal. Then I put a star at the top of the page to remind myself to go back there and transpose whatever I've written there into the project I'm working on. For example, I recently wrote about how I'm understanding the relationship between a character and myself. I might say, "Well this character is really my aunt Peggy," and then I might write about my aunt Peggy a little bit.

Mother-Daughter Diary

I love Peter Stillman's ideas in *Families Writing* where he talks about having a journal on the dining room table. People can write in it as they pass by, and it becomes a history of the family over the years. When Sarah and I went to England we kept a joint diary. I bought a diary with maps. It looked like the perfect travel diary. I wrote in it lots, and once in a while Sarah would ask for it. We took turns, although there wasn't any rule about it. When we went to Stonehenge, we each drew pictures in the diary and wrote about the experience. It is a great treasure to have.

For the few months before Sarah went off to college, perhaps from May to September, I kept a journal of our life together. I wrote on the computer so I could print it out for her. I just wanted to record what our days were like when we still lived together. I was writing specifically for my daughter as a going-off-to-college present. Usually, I tend to write with no one in mind except myself.

Journal Companions

When I read the diaries of Louisa May Alcott I noticed that she did something interesting. At the end of each month she reread her diary entries and summarized her month. She inspired me to go back and read all of my old diaries. I wrote a couple sentences summarizing them, thinking I would make an overview of my whole life. Since I have dozens of diaries it takes a long time to read them. The project turned out to be too overwhelming.

I'm teaching a journal class right now at my local library. In the first class I read excerpts from the journals of Samuel Pepys and Andy Warhol, who were the same kind of journal writer. They wrote gossip and exactly what their day was like—down to the details, to what they did every minute. In the second class, when I talk about making a choice for solitude, I intro-duce the journals of May Sarton and a Frenchman who sailed across the Pacific Ocean. In the third class I talk about things that we don't have choices about. I read from the journal of a gay man who wrote during the Depression and from the jour-nal of a man who is blind. In the first class I have the partici-pants write about their lives and try to take a keepsake from each day. Then in the second class, I ask them to think about their lives and be conscious about choices they've made or what choices they're making. In the third class we talk and write about some things you don't have choices about, things you just have to go with. I thought people would be shy about sharing their journals, but they're not.

Read at Your Own Risk

I've heard so many stories about parents reading their children's diaries that I think kids need to come up with ideas about where to hide their diaries and how to keep them private. I don't hide mine from my daughter, but I told her to read them at her own risk. My diaries take up an entire book shelf, from one end of the room to the other. There are dozens, three or four just from recent years. I put them on the top shelf so nobody will pick them up idly and browse through. Except for Sarah, I really don't welcome, I don't invite anybody to read them.

The Professional Diary

I keep a separate file on my computer where I talk about what's going on with projects and editors. Mostly I talk about my worries—am I going to be able to finish this and I want to finish it and what am I going to send to Patti, my editor. John Steinbeck kept a journal while he was writing *East of Eden*, published as *Journal of a Novel: The East of Eden Letters*. Every morning he would write an unsent letter to his editor in which he would discuss life issues as well as ideas for the book. I did that while I was writing *Levittown*. That's separate from my regular diaries, though. I always feel so pressed for time that I'm reluctant to spend too much time on that type of journal writing. When I'm writing a novel, even my diaries are sketchy. I don't get into much detail or let too much emotion out because I want to do that in the novel.

Stephen Trimble

"A Personal Library of My Past"

Young Stephen Trimble

When speaking to audiences about the process of writing natural history, author and photographer Stephen Timble shares passages from his journal to illustrate how impressions from the field breathe spirit into his books and essays. On May 22 and 23, 1982, Trimble camps in the Black Rock Desert in Nevada while researching *The Sagebrush Ocean: A Natural History of the Great Basin*. In his journal he captures sensory impressions of this "incredible, unearthly," landscape:

> "The basin is so damn big. This feels like a whole earth, this one playa . . . It's an interesting juxtaposition of level and angle—the knife line of the rim of the playa circling (wheeling)

round at eye level, the narrow band of sharp angled mountains just above, a great dome of blue haze, and below the flat mosaic of mud . . .
Silent lifeless clay for miles."

Next, Trimble narrates the sunrise:

"Sunrise—the clay goes from gray-blue to gray to deep tan just after sunup. Lots of detail at first—the cracks all casting shadows. Then the color warms as the sun gets higher—yellows—and distances begin to get funny—the mountains recede into the haze and begin to float . . . Sunrise here takes a long time—the openness does it. From first color to actual sunrise takes hours, it seems."

In a brief entry, Trimble catalogues the assortment of campers with him on the playa:

"Interesting population of campers in places like this—rock hounds (retired folks), ORV/bikers (red necks), and seekers after the ultimate desert (environmentalist, ecofreak, observing, experience-hungry, quiet, crazy, desert rats)."

For Trimble, describing mountains and deserts in images and metaphors, right there in the field, is imperative. When he begins composing a piece for publication, he opens his journal, relives the immediacy of experience, and transforms his notes into art.

Trimble confesses a sympathy with Native American people in thinking of the world as alive and regarding the sun and moon as very powerful forces in our lives. In the field he listens to the landscape and looks as hard as he can. As Trimble opens himself to the world around him, the spirit of the land flows through him and into his journal. On April 27, 1987, Trimble hikes the Tsegi Canyon in Arizona and catches its colors, sounds, and movements in his journal. All the while he imagines ancient Anasazi life in "his" fictional village for his children's book *The Village of Blue Stone:*

"I've climbed east from Tsegi Overlook to a rocky point . . . The views are green, orange and blue. The junipers are much yellower than the piñon. They are so bright and clumpy, they look like blossoms amongst grass . . . I'm here on retreat from my village. A guest. The wind is cool, the sun hot. I hear chickadees in the piñons as I walk past, a male deer bounds stiff-legged over a rise and disappears—white rump the whitest thing for miles . . ."

To Trimble landscape is home, not merely an object for research. With the birth of his children, Dory and Jacob, he began looking at the land in a fresh way—slower, closer up. On camping trips and family hikes, he traded seeing miles and miles of new landscape for the even longer view of helping his children feel at home in natural settings. Through these experiences, he and his wife hope that the earth will become "a source of strength and sustenance, a dependable spiritual bedrock" for their children.

Like his geologist father who taught him to pay attention to the land, Trimble guides his two children to form a connection with landscape. He takes them to canyons and mountains, where they watch for rainbows, full moons, burrows, beetles, leaves, and feathers. "As parents," he writes in "Sing Me Down the Mountain" (from *The Geography of Childhood),* our job is to pay attention, to create possibilities—to be careful matchmakers between our children and the Earth."

Trimble started taking his daughter on field trips, just the two of them, when she was six years old and he was on assignment, photographing a book about Nevada. Jennifer Owings Dewey had given Dory a lovely sketchbook. She couldn't write a complete sentence, but her father encouraged her to draw. He took dictation as she told him what it was like on the trip in Nevada.

"As children," he writes in *"A Land of One's Own"* (*The Geography of Childhood),* "we need time to wander, to be outside, to nibble on icicles and watch ants, to build with dirt and sticks in a hollow of the earth, to lie back and contemplate clouds and chickadees . . ."

Trying to articulate one's adventures in the natural world on the page of a journal is more than a way to understand experience. For Stephen Trimble journal writing is making a connection to home.

Stephen Trimble's books include

The Village of Blue Stone

The Sagebrush Ocean: A Natural History of the Great Basin

The People: Indians of the American Southwest

Words from the Land: Encounters with Natural History Writing (editor)

The Geography of Childhood: Why Children Need Wild Places, with Gary Paul Nabhan

Testimony: Writers of the West Speak on Behalf of Utah Wilderness, compiled with Terry Tempest Williams

The Interview

I started writing for publication in the early 1970s when I was a park ranger. I didn't keep a journal in those days. I'm amazed now that I could have written those small early books without one. I was only minimally employed so I worked on one project at a time. I'd sign a contract, complete the fieldwork, and go directly from hiking and photographing to my typewriter. In essence, the first draft was my journal.

Journal keeping became an important part of my life as I began working on longer books. After 1980, my life as a free-lance writer became complicated by more commitments. Fieldwork might not be immediately translated into a draft. It became clear that I needed to start keeping better records.

I finally buckled down to keeping notes consistently when I began research for my *Great Basin* book in 1982. For the first time I needed to research a full-length book about a huge piece of landscape rather than a single national park. It became crucial to get down in my journal my immediate responses to the landscape—sensory impressions, images, and metaphors. I wanted that immediacy to draw on when I turned to the writing.

Telling Details, Telling Phrases

Describing the landscape right then and there, not trying to conjure it back from memory, from a distance, is critical if you're going to write vivid natural history. When the telling details reveal themselves, you've got to record them: a turkey vulture feather twirling down from the sky in the fog and getting caught in a spider web, or the exact rhythm of a canyon wren's calls in the red rock canyons of southern Utah or a loon's cry on a lake in Maine.

The other crucial aspect of my journal grows from interviewing. I've worked for fifteen years with Indian people in the Southwest, writing a series of interview-based books. In my text, I let native people speak for themselves. At first I recorded the interviews and later transcribed them. But I became so bogged down in transcription I gave up and started taking notes and listening for the telling phrases—just as I listen to the land for telling details.

I visit someone and, with luck, they invite me in. We sit at the kitchen table. I scribble in my journal. I have a good memory and Indian people are comfortable with silences. Using a journal is a very different kind of invasion of space than switching on a tape recorder.

I want to hear people's stories. I'm not a trained anthropologist with theories to prove. The stories may be true or they may be exaggerated. They may even be outright lies. In the end it really doesn't matter. What I want to know is what people want me to know. When I'm listening to someone, I'm listening for those phrases I'm going to use in the book. It's exhilarating when someone says something distinct and powerful about an aspect of the lives I'm writing about. I can hear it. It's a physical sensation. I star the phrase in my journal.

Pondering My Life

Sometimes I have the urge to ponder my own life, but I make no effort to do that kind of journal writing with any regularity. I tend to do it on airplanes, when I'm leaving my life and going off to begin an adventure or to give a talk.

Years ago, when I was involved in difficult relationships and when I was single and lonesome, I would write about my life. Now that I am happily married and my life brim-full with family and predictability, I don't tend to write those yearning analytic, self-exploratory kinds of things. I might write about how I feel about my aging parents or the wonder of seeing my children growing up, but it's more outward-directed.

Journal Indexes

I use nine-by-seven blue exam books from university bookstores. They cost about four bucks and have 120 numbered, lined pages. They look humble, not intimidating the way a leather-bound hand-made book can appear. Everything goes in there: thoughts on my own life, notes on interviews and lectures, book titles my friends recommend.

After I've filled up a blue book, I take the time to sit down at my computer and index it in a fairly simple fashion. For interviews, it's just the person's name and the page numbers in the journal where the notes occur. I'll put his or her name, the tribe or place or project, and the date. This allows me to click on the index and use search commands to find anything. So if I'm writing away about the Southwest, for example, and I remember that one particular person said something eloquent about their homeland or pueblo and all I remember is a name, I simply search the computer index for that name. Bingo. The machine tells me exactly which page in which journal I need. If I can't remember the name, I search for the tribal name or place name. Either way, I can quickly defuse my frustration with my aging brain's blank spots.

Hand-Written Intimacy

Rather than hauling a notebook computer with me, I'm partial to the hand-written journal. There's something quite magical about spilling words onto the screen, right out of your brain. It's a very different experience to write with a pen over paper, and I value both greatly. The point of the journal is to make your thoughts as immediate and personal, as intimate and free as possible. There's something elemental about using a pen on paper in the sunlight out there in the mountains or desert.

When I'm hiking, I'll pull out my journal when I stop for rest, open myself up to the world around me, and listen and look as hard as I can. When I start to enter phrases, I allow myself to be whimsical and crazy. I start writing and see what happens. Later I'll use the good stuff and forget about the junk.

I try to use letter-writing language. If I want to be humorous and make bad jokes, I go right ahead. It's unlikely any of this will be used in a finished piece, but sometimes it will. If I want to be a little sappy I don't worry about it, and if I want to be profane I don't worry about it. It's very much an unedited, uncensored style that often leads me to useful phrases buried between self-indulgent jokes and silly metaphors. These rantings also lead me into an openness—to emotion and passion. This grant of freedom in my journal keeps me creative rather than restrained and refined and academic.

Journal as Physical Memory

There's a beauty to being both a photographer and writer. When the light is wonderful and I'm in a remarkable place, or when I'm taking portraits of people, I react actively to the world. I see graphics and design, I sense mood. It happens decisively, in a moment, between me and the land or the light or the person.

Writing in my journal is much more contemplative. When I'm describing the landscape, I'm doing my best to articulate in words what I see and feel. My journal is a physical memory, the record-

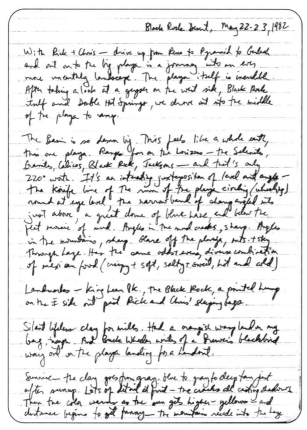

From Stephen Trimble's journal

ing of the very best that I can give to a particular situation with my own sensibilities. It's a unique personal library of my past.

Technology intercedes when I take a photograph. The picture is preserved on film, then printed. Theoretically it should be a more powerful statement of a moment, but the technology makes it less personal than writing. The photographs are farther away from my own experience.

I have enormous affection for my journal because it records those moments of excitement when I'm learning something brand new, whether it's seeing something I've never seen before in a landscape or capturing in words a sound, a color, or a vision of a storm. Here lie the records of those moments when I'm listening to someone and all of a sudden some new comprehension clicks. Because it is an extraordinarily dependable friend—good at both listening and responding—my journal, more than my file of photographs, is the place I preserve the sweetest moments of my life.

Source Book

Another thing I like to record is quotes. Copying them out and responding to them often leads to the seed of an essay, the perfect phrase or a book title. Writing down a quote gives it more weight than underlining the same words. It's very much like making your own maps. I love maps and truly believe that the only way to really understand the lay of the land is to draw out your own map of the place—even if you only trace from a published map. It teaches you something about the way the land fits together in much the same way that copying out a quote teaches the way the words in a passage fit together.

Writing and Praying at the End of the Day

In 1995 Terry Tempest Williams and I edited a book of essays by twenty western writers dedicated to saving wilderness in Utah—a book called *Testimony: Writers of the West Speak on Behalf of Utah Wilderness.* We asked our contributors, who write about the West and the idea of wilderness, to pour out their hearts in short essays. Terry and I went to Washington to present this book to Congress and spent two days lobbying in the House and Senate. At the end of the first exhausting day, with an hour or so open between intensive lobbying and dinner, we gravitated to the reading room at the Library of Congress. It seemed like the absolutely perfect refuge for writers—our version of finding a place to pray or attending evening Mass. We didn't plan it. It just happened.

What did we do? We sat quietly in that monumental space dedicated to words and wrote in our journals.

Sara Holbrook

"Going to My Writing Place"

Sara Holbrook, age 8

"Many writers feel guilty about spending too much time doodling," says performance poet Sara Holbrook. "I'm just the opposite. Even with all those journals on the shelf, I always feel guilty that I haven't taken enough notes, haven't gotten it all down in my journals."

Like an investigative reporter, Holbrook trains her eye on the details of her world. She searches out sights, sounds, and smells—a squished squirrel, a clanking flagpole, the ripe air of zoo cages—and translates these images into notes and phrases. She dashes them down on the index cards she carries in her wallet. Back home, she transfers these observations into her journal, where they incubate, sometimes for years, until she revisits them and spins them into poems.

Holbrook calls her journal a toxic waste dump for the frustrations and angers she doesn't want to air in public. On the private page, she engages in self-talk to gain perspective. "When things happen to me," she confesses, "part of me reacts as an adolescent, part as an adult." Rather than punching someone, she deposits these emotional thrashings into her journal. Here they simmer and smolder until they ignite her stash of images. From this mixture—notes reflecting a wide range of feelings and observations—come her powerful poems about significant issues facing preteens and adolescents—divorce, anger, violence, love, friendship, and self-esteem.

Holbrook began writing poems for her daughters Katie and Kelly in order to record the joys and trials of their growing up. She entered them in a journal that she left open on the dining room table, inviting the girls to respond. First they drew simple line drawings to illustrate their mother's poems. Later they vented verbal storms of fury and wrote poems of their own. This family journal evolved into a problem-solving device as sharing poetry became a way of sharing understanding. When one daughter expressed fear about the tooth fairy and didn't want it coming into her room, Holbrook's poem, "The Tooth Comes Out," helped her laugh about her concern. The family journal gave Holbrook and her daughters a way to talk about difficult issues—bad hair days, obsessions with body shape and size, feelings of being left out and lonely—and drew them closer together.

When it comes to journal keeping, privacy rules the Holbrook home. If the journal is closed, no peeking. An open book is open season. Katie and Kelly, now grown, have always respected this practice. Holbrook writes from a very personal space, deep inside. Any violation of that privacy would prod her to write in code and devise exotic ways of hiding her journal. During a school visit, a child asked her if anyone had ever read her journal. It had happened to him and he thought she should write a poem about it. So she did.

"PRIVATE PARTS"

You read MY journal?
Off MY shelf?
MY dreams placed undercover?
Conversations with MY self?
That's where I get to yell
and no one's yelling back.
Where I reach my hand out
and know it won't get smacked.
That's where I go for confidence.
Where I can practice and rehearse.
My spot out of the spotlight.
Where no one tells me not to curse.
I thought I was playing safely.
You peeped.
It's where my thoughts reside.
You thief.
You should have knocked
and let me dress and come outside.

From Sara Holbrook's family journal

Holbrook speaks at more than one hundred schools annually, holding writing workshops for students and leading teacher-training workshops. She watches the faces of her audience as she acts out the emotions of her poems. Teachers and librarians have told her that some of her poems are too angry, but Holbrook believes that expressing feelings in words—in poetry or in a journal—is the best place to go with them.

"If kids do not learn this lesson, or do not have access to good language skills to express feelings, what other weapon will they choose?" she asks. "The alternatives are scary."

Sara Holbrook's books include

The Dog Ate My Homework
Am I Naturally This Crazy?
I Never Said I Wasn't Difficult
Which Way to the Dragon!
Nothing's the End of the World
Chicks Up Front (for adults)

The Interview

When I was in high school I kept a diary, which was really a record of who I was dating. Looking back, it is an amazing account of who I kissed, who looked at me on what day. It's terrible. I was so boy crazy.

I wanted to write about other things, but in my family it wasn't safe. I always had the feeling that things weren't right at home. We had a lot of problems around my mother's alcoholism, but I never wrote about it. My sister did, however, and when my mother read her diary, she destroyed it.

I always had the sense that I wanted to be a writer, but it was beyond my scope of comprehension. I didn't know writers were real people. I remember sitting at my desk, pen in hand, organizing papers, thinking what I would be was a secretary.

Any writing dreams I may have had were set back even further when I got booted out of accelerated English in the eighth grade.

Poet as Journalist

I write poetry like a reporter. I'm always looking for things outside of myself and taking notes about them. I have gone through life taking notes. The first time I clearly recall doing that is when John F. Kennedy was shot. I was in geometry class. I remember reaching into my desk and taking out a small notebook. As they were talking over the PA system, I sat and jotted down notes.

My journal is stuffed with notes that I've taken at different places. I carry index cards in my wallet for that purpose. Then I transpose my observations into my journal. Some of the ideas I develop: I'll recreate the scene or make comments about it; others I just transfer. It may take years before my notes end up in a poem, if at all.

One time I was working out in the yard and I picked up a little bird that had fallen out of its nest and put it back. Plop. It fell out again. I put it back. Plop. Back. Plop. Back. Three or four times. Then I had this warm feeling on my arm and I looked down to discover the bird had given me lice. I went into the house, took a brush and scrubbed my arm. All the time I thought, there's got to be a poem in here somewhere.

In my journal I jotted down how I'd tried to be a good Samaritan of nature and in return the bird gave me lice. Six years later I wrote a poem about saying gross things at the dinner table entitled "May I Be Excused?"

> At dinner she said
> "Nice cat, is he yours?"
>
> "Yeah, he is," I said.
> "He hardly gets fur balls at all.
> When he does?
> He goes right outside to spit.

And he eats all his food.
'fore the maggots get it,
most times."

I said, "Pass the rice.

"Once a dead squirrel
was behind the garage—
no one's fault, natural causes.
It was twelve times its size
'cause it swelled from the heat?
Kids came and saw it
(ten cents a peek),
but the maggots got it
after a week or so, really sick."
I said, "Pass the meat.

"One summer
the trash cans got maggots
so bad I thought I would vomit.
So I called my dad,
who cleaned them himself
with a poison
he keeps on the shelf.
He said if I touched it
my fingers would melt."

I said, "Pass the milk.

"I once touched a bird and got lice."

She put down her fork
and just said,
"How nice."

I have at least twenty journals, all different. Some are corny looking, some trendy. I like writing on graph paper and using art sketchbooks. Many writers feel guilty about spending too much time doodling. I'm just the opposite. Even with all those journals on the shelf, I always feel guilty that I haven't taken enough notes, haven't gotten it all down in my journals. I wish I'd written more about my kids.

Privacy Rule

When I write in my journal I'm writing from a place way inside of me. It's a physical presence, a very private space, where I go to write. If I didn't know my journal was safe, I'd come up with exotic ways of hiding it.

I use my journal for self-talk, a way to gain perspective when I'm frustrated. Writing it down helps me sort things out. It helps me keep my feet on the ground and my head going the right way. It's also a place I go to dump toxic waste, which is why it would be so unfair for somebody to come along and read it. I'm afraid somebody would look at my journals and say, "She was really rather shallow and petty wasn't she?" When things happen to me, part of me reacts as an adolescent, part as an adult. That's another reason why my journals are embarrassing. The frustrations and anger I don't want to drag out in public I leave behind in my journal. I learned a long time ago that it's a good place to take those feelings, rather than punching your boss.

In my home we have a rule: if you put something on a piece of paper and leave it open on the table, it's open season. But if you put it in a book and close the book, then nobody's allowed to look. My kids have always respected that, and I've respected it for them.

On-line Journaling

Writing on the computer is much faster for me. I have a few friends and authors I E-mail about my daily activities, joys and frustrations—my daughter getting married, my dog getting hit by a car. I dump copies of my letters into Word Perfect files. Once a month I print them out and put them into a file. When I lost all of my September correspondence because I didn't save things correctly, I felt like someone had stolen one of my children. I'm more careful now.

When I couldn't find a dress for my daughter's wedding and

I didn't want to go looking like one of the Lennon Sisters, I complained to Sharon Draper in an E-mail, and as a joke she sent me a picture of a dress from a 1972 Spiegel catalogue. It was the ugliest dress I'd ever seen, but on the back of the page was a man in a leisure suit, hair falling over his eyes in a curl, really obnoxious, but very 1970s.

I sent her an E-mail that began, "Well wrap me in ruffles and curl my hair, if this isn't the best thing I've ever seen" and yack, yack, yack. The first line of that letter turned into a poem about ordering men out of a catalog, which has since turned into one of my crowd pleaser performance pieces for adults.

> "Well, wrap me in ruffles and curl my hair
> Will you look at that one on page two.
> Not the dress. Not the dress, but that dream-feed
>   in denim,
> That one, shoes pictured on page 56."

Family Journal

Journal keeping has drawn us very close together as a family. In a journal kept open on the table—remember our privacy rule—I would write poems based on my observations and my children would add line drawings. When my daughter was in kindergarten, I accompanied her class to the zoo. It occurred to me that nobody even looked at the animals. I came home and wrote this poem:

> "The trip to the zoo
> was crummy, because
> the reindeer were home
> but not Santa Claus.
>
> I found a pine cone,
> a pretty good stick,
> fences to climb,
> and railing to lick.

But then just about
got smothered by stink
and I walked for a year
to get something to drink.

If you go to the zoo
take plenty of hours,
But don't touch the toilets
or pick any flowers."

I used the journal to help my kids solve problems, too. My daughter was afraid of the tooth fairy. She didn't want the tooth fairy coming into her room in the middle of the night, stealing her tooth, scaring her out of her skin, no way. So I wrote a poem about it and she was able to laugh about the tooth fairy.

As they got older, I continued writing for them. When my one daughter was having a bad hair year and was feeling kind of pudgy (I didn't think she was pudgy), she looked at me with tears in her eyes and said, "I hate my body." I wrote her an I-hate-my-body poem. It's the way we ended up talking about things.

Very often I would write at night after the kids went to bed and the house was quiet. One night I walked the dog past the school and heard a flagpole clanking in the wind. That's really a lonely sound, I thought. I came home, sat down at the kitchen table, and wrote a poem about being lonely. I left the journal open.

I'm not going steady. I'm nobody's friend.
I guess I'm about the loneliest of anybody.
There's no one waiting at the door at three for me to meet
And if I'm late for lunch no one saves me a seat.
My love life's not the topic of hot homeroom conversation.
This school's made up of partners, two halves to every whole
Except me left on the outside like that clanking old flag pole.

The next morning my oldest daughter, who was in middle school at the time, came down for breakfast. As she ate her bowl of Cheerios, she pulled the poem over and read it. She was furious. She came screaming into the next room, "Why did you write that poem about me? You're not going to read that one to anybody, are you?" I knew that this time I had written a real poem, one that made someone else say "I feel that way, too."

Then my children started writing their own poems. There's a tender one by my daughter, written when she was thirteen, entitled "Separation."

> Separation is when bubble gum is pulled off your lips.
> Separation is when your favorite ball falls out of your mitts.
> But the worst separation is when the two most favorite people
> Have arguments and fits
> Even with all your advice and tips
> It all comes out to the worst separation ever.

Our tradition of sharing feelings in our family journal gave the kids permission to talk about difficult issues, like their parents' divorce.

Real-Life Advice

I write about real-life topics like divorce and anger and I encourage school kids to use their journals and poetry to express all different kinds of feelings. I show them how I've used my journal to write about significant events, some happy, some not so happy, because life isn't like it is on *Home Improvement*. They all nod. They know. I tell them how it was when my dog died or what it was like growing up with an alcoholic mother. I tell them that sometimes they will have to hide their writing and that's OK. I encourage them strongly to be information gatherers and to describe their environment. Then they can attach their feelings to images, which is, after all, the stuff of poetry. I write from the outside in. I have to get the images fixed in my head before I can use them in a poem. The journal is my place to capture those images in phrases and notes.

Richard Ammon

"One Writer's Laboratory"

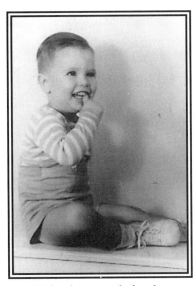

Richard Ammon before he
could write

In a refinished room in the basement of his home, Richard Ammon pursues two activities that he believes keep him in sound mental health. Here he writes in an old-fashioned composition book, the journal he carries back and forth between home and his office at Penn State-Harrisburg where he is an associate professor of elementary education. It is also where, for a half-hour every day, faithfully, asking not to be interrupted, he closes the door and practices his four-valved, double-bored, upright euphonium, a brass instrument with tonal qualities between a trombone and French horn.

One night a week Ammon arrives, euphonium in hand, at the

Trinity Lutheran Church in Camp Hill, Pennsylvania, to make music. Seven quasi-serious male musicians, plus their director, perform during church services. Sometimes, for a modest fee, the group also plays at community gigs like convocations or arts award ceremonies. If needed, they can even turn into a pep band.

Although Ammon began lessons at ten and has been playing for more than forty years, music is his hobby. A college music major for a short time, he decided there was a limit to his musical ability and made the decision to pursue teaching and writing.

As both musician and author, Ammon understands the value of having the time and space to experiment. The same playful spirit found in jazz improvisation, one of his interests, can be seen in his journal writing. Between the covers of inexpensive notebooks, Ammon doodles, records the details of daily life, blows off steam, makes discoveries, and works through the challenges of professional writing.

Charting his struggles with manuscripts and editors reassures Ammon that quandaries are a recurring, perhaps predictable, part of the writing process. For example, on May 31, 1994, he was still groping to resolve with his editor a dilemma concerning his picture book *An Amish Christmas*. "Received my Amish Christmas manuscript back from Marcia. She doesn't like it! She's probably right, of course. She's saying make it for younger children, or make it for older children. And reduce the school program! I thought I had." Reading back through these entries when new barriers appear reminds Ammon that he has successfully negotiated compositional roadblocks before, a realization that encourages new projects.

Always interested in arriving at a definition of himself, Ammon explores on the pages of his journal connections between the observational and personal. "As I read back over my old journals, I can see raw emotions. Now the attic of my brain is too cluttered to invite guests, but what I do see coming out of this tangle is an evolution of my thinking."

His journal entries reflect his relationships with his wife and daughters and his career as teacher and writer. They also capture his observations from the daily and mundane side of life, such as the subtleties of crabgrass. Sharpening his powers of observation as the lawn mower of the family, Ammon has developed such an intimate relationship with the weed that jocular references to pre-, season of, and post-crabgrass, rather than the calendar terms spring and summer, dominate how he views the seasons and how he dates journal entries.

Ammon writes in his journal primarily when he feels compelled to capture the joyous or sad moments of life or when he wants to have a private conversation with himself. When he is upset about something, writing helps him understand his feelings. When he needs to confront someone, he sets down in his journal the concrete points he needs to air and often discovers a path toward resolution.

A brass player's mouth muscles are so finely tuned, Ammon says, that if he doesn't practice every day for at least fifteen minutes he notices diminishing skill. If he misses three days, his wife notices. If he misses a week, his audience notices. That's how it is in public arenas, but—fortunately—journal writing is private: nobody else notices lapses there.

Richard Ammon's books include

Growing Up Amish
Trains at Work
An Amish Christmas
An Amish Wedding
The Kids Book of Chocolate
The Story of Ourselves with Michael Tunnell (for adults)

The Interview

I have no clue how I got started keeping a journal. But there are two reasons that journal writing is important to me. First, it is therapeutic. When I am upset about something, writing helps me understand exactly how I feel. Sometimes I'll know I'm upset, but I won't be clear until I write down exactly how I feel about the problem.

When instances occur where I need to confront someone, I write in my journal to set down direct, concrete points I need to make. This prethinking has allowed me to keep on track, and that often leads to resolution. Other times, the writing is simply to blow off steam.

Secondly, journal writing captures moments of my life. I carry my journal back and forth between home and school. I write in these marbly-covered books that seem like throwbacks to the old composition books I had in elementary school. The disadvantage, of course, is that if you rip out a page, you often lose its cousin at the other end of the book. The moments can be joyous or sad. For example, our quietly celebrated twenty-fifth wedding anniversary became almost spiritually significant to me.

Observational Record

Perhaps my wife and perhaps my writing have taught me to become a better observer. For example, I've begun to notice seasons within seasons. My nose knows that spring begins long before everything turns lush and green when trees burst with invisible clouds of pollen to the winds. I know when summer is coming because these pale green spikes, the harbinger of crabgrass, poke up through the lawn. Deeper into the summer as the crabgrass dies out, yellow jacket season arrives, which lasts until the first frost.

Observational to Personal

I'm always interested in arriving at a definition of myself, so I explore connections between the observational and the personal. A journal entry might begin along one line of thinking and shift into quite another. Just like a conversation with a friend can jump and shift, so, too, does a conversation with myself.

As I read back over my old journals, I can see raw emotion. Now the attic of my brain is too cluttered to invite guests, but what I do see coming out of this tangle is an evolution of my thinking. My entries are peppered with reflections about my relationship with my wife, my daughters, my teaching, my writing, and me. There are numerous entries where I have expressed the pain I've felt for others. Recently I identified so greatly with the suffering of those parents whose sons and daughters on a study-abroad trip lost their lives aboard TWA Flight 800.

Handle with Care

In my college classes I talk about the importance of journals and how a teacher can kill the whole thing, too. I write with my students and show them that I still keep one. Some well-intentioned teachers regiment their classes: "OK everybody, now write in your journals for the next ten minutes." So here's journal time, and what do the kids put down? Something to fill the ten minutes and please the teacher. That is not serving the kids very well. I would invite children to write in their journals, not require it.

Part of the beauty of keeping a journal is making discoveries. Sharing these discoveries gives children ideas about the kinds of inventions their classmates are making. Nobody should be required to share, but there ought to be a time for sharing. When a shy student finally gets comfortable enough to share, he or she needs gentle, receiving comments about the work because early on children tend to take criticism personally.

> May 31, 1994
>
> Received my Amish Christmas manuscript back from Marcia. She doesn't like it! She's probably right, of course.
>
> My question is — what do you want to know about Christmas?
> My original idea was Henry's trying to learn his part — that was the story.
> She's saying make it for younger children, or make it for older children.
>
> And reduce the school program! I thought I had. If I reduce the school program, what's the point?
>
> Ok Maybe one story is Henry's school Christmas Program (better title)
>
> The other is an Amish Christmas. But what makes that different than what's in GROWING UP AMISH?
>
> This was my throw-away story among Henry's Run-Away/ horse.

Richard Ammon uses his journal to resolve problems

Writer's Laboratory

Did you ever ask an artist to explain something to you? He or she immediately picks up a pad and pencil and starts drawing. Whether you're an athlete or a musician, anybody doing something creative, you need space and time to experiment. The journal is a small part of the writer's laboratory. It's the arena where the writer can experiment, the place to monkey around. It's very private doodling. It's primitive, my id on paper. I have never once thought that someone might pick up my journal. In my home we don't invade each other's privacy.

Manuscript Muddles

There is a connection between writing, thinking, and the unconscious. Sometimes I work out in my journal problems I'm having with a manuscript. I was surprised to read my entry on May 31, 1994. I was still struggling with *An Amish Christmas*. (I thought I had resolved this dilemma by then.) Nevertheless, here I was groping:

> Received my Amish Christmas manuscript back from Marcia. She doesn't like it! She's probably right, of course.
>
> My question is—What do you want to know about Christmas?
>
> My original idea was Henry's trying to learn his part—that was the story.
>
> She's saying make it for younger children, or make it for older children.
>
> And reduce the school program! I thought I had. If I reduce the school program, what's the point?
>
> OK. Maybe one story is *Henry's School Christmas Program*. (better title)
>
> The other is an Amish Christmas. But what makes that different than what's in *Growing Up Amish*?
>
> This was my throw-away story among Henry's Run-Away horse.

What's interesting is seeing this muddle and being able to remind myself where I was before I resolved this quandary. What's reassuring is knowing that you've been there before, knowing that these struggles are merely part of the process and if there's any good stuff there, it will emerge.

Lynne Cherry

"Reality Check"

Young Lynne Cherry on the beach

In *A River Ran Wild*, author, illustrator, and environmental activist Lynne Cherry tells the story of Marion Stoddart of Groton, Massachusetts, a spry 63-year-old woman whose dedication and energy reclaimed the health of the long-abused Nashua River. When Stoddart set out to establish a greenbelt along the river, she was told by state officials that Massachusetts wasn't interested in buying land along such a filthy waterway. Stoddart organized the Nashua River Cleanup Committee and campaigned for laws to prevent mills and factories from dumping chemicals, dyes, and waste into the water. She sent politicians bottles of polluted river water and asked businessmen to help convince paper companies to build a treatment plant. She cleared away garbage, spoke at town meetings, and lobbied for laws to protect all rivers. The result: in 1966 Massachusetts passed a state Clean Water Act.

During her research for *A River Ran Wild*, Cherry canoed the Nasuha River with Stoddart. Later, by car, they explored the nearby countryside so Cherry could sketch in her journal and record the details of Stoddart's battle to reclaim the river. Cherry's book is a tribute to Stoddart, a caring visionary whose life work profoundly influenced the author.

Cherry had also been deeply touched by the life and murder in 1988 of Chico Mendes, a rubber tapper, who launched an international campaign to draw attention to the destruction of the Brazilian rain forest. Journal in hand, Cherry traveled to the Amazon rain forest to research *The Great Kapok Tree*. This book, which is dedicated to his memory, captures in sumptuous illustrations the complex ecosystem of the rain forest Mendes died to preserve. For all the creatures who call it home—toucan, macaw, tree frog, jaguar, porcupine, anteater, three-toed sloth—Cherry inspires readers to respect the rain forest and take action to protect it.

In 1992 Cherry's goal of connecting children to both the natural world and books about the environment led her to establish the Center for Children's Environmental Literature. More than two hundred children's authors and illustrators work together to increase environmental awareness and action among teachers and children.

Each edition of CCEL's newsletter, *Nature's Course*, presents creative and inspiring ways to use children's books as a resource for teaching about a specific environmental topic. For example, an issue on rivers and watersheds highlights Cherry's *A River Ran Wild*, Thomas Locker's *Where the River Begins*, and Holling Clancy Holling's *Paddle-to-the-Sea*, and offers suggested activities on cleaning up local rivers and ideas for using river study to integrate curriculum. A regular feature of *Nature's*

Course describes what children across the country have been doing to make the world a better place.

Lynne Cherry was drawn to nature from the time she was a young girl. Hers was a passion barely understood by neighborhood playmates. Soon, her journal became her best friend, the place where she sketched the outdoors and made up stories.

Recently Cherry reread her journals, which she began keeping at the age of eight, for one specific purpose—to answer the question, "How have I evolved?" Recorded in more than fifty volumes are her entries about environmental activists who, like Marion Stoddart and Chico Mendes, have influenced her development. "I thought I got my values through osmosis, but it's very obvious that I've had these momentous moments when someone has had a great influence on me." This discovery inspires Cherry to write and illustrate environmental books for children in hopes that she, in turn, will incite them to respect and protect the land.

Wilderness tugs at Cherry constantly, and periodic trips into the field to research books are not enough to satisfy her longing to connect to the environment that sustains her. Cherry needs to be outdoors daily, caking her boots with snow or mud. Recently relocated from Washington, D.C., to the Catoctin Mountains in Maryland, Cherry remains stunned by the beauty of nature. "I go out the door at night and absolute silence hits me. I can see the sky, the stars, the fronts moving in, the weather." Her fifty-two acre farm abuts ten thousand acres of state and national forest. Into this wilderness, Cherry takes her journal, sometimes just to sketch and write for her own enjoyment, with no fear of messing up and no pressure to produce.

Lynne Cherry's books include

The Great Kapok Tree: A Tale of the Amazon Rain Forest
The River Ran Wild: An Environmental History
The Armadillo from Amarillo
The Dragon and the Unicorn

Flute's Journey: The Life of a Wood Thrush
The Shaman's Apprentice: A Tale of the Amazon Rain Forest with
Mark Plotkin

The Interview

I wrote every day, all through my teens, from age eight to my
early twenties, in little books with lined paper that my dad got
me from a pharmaceutical company. There was a book for
every month, and I'd have to write really small. I'd
include photographs and illustrations and always decorate the
cover. I don't know where I got the idea to keep a journal. My
mom said I wrote and drew from the time I was a little kid
when I stapled paper together to make books. When I was a

Lynne Cherry's sketch of Machu Picchu

A village in Suriname, South America

teenager I would go to my room after dinner, close the door, and write for half an hour instead of doing my homework. I didn't have to hide my journals or lock them up because I could trust my parents. In my twenties life started to get more exciting and full.

I find it relaxing to sketch in my journal, without the pressure of researching a book. It gives me the freedom to be creative; it doesn't matter if I mess up. I write in my journal when I'm happy or when exciting things are happening. I write when I'm having an adventure. When I'm traveling I write very frequently, almost daily. When I'm home working on a book and not a whole lot is happening, I don't write as much.

I also write a lot of letters and correspond with quite a few people. I often copy the letters into my journal. I corresponded with Dr. Seuss up until his death. I've framed all his letters. If my house were burning down I'd run and get them.

Reality Check

Whenever I have a crisis, I guess once every five years, I go back to my journals to try to figure out what's going on with me. I get back into my mind as a ten-year-old or a teenager or a woman in her early twenties. I see myself doing the same things over and over again. I hadn't realized until I picked up a journal from age eighteen that certain patterns were already established back then.

There's just no way I could remember, but it's all there—how I felt and the things I was going through. Now in my forties when I'm trying to figure out how I turned out this way, I read back over my life and it hits me—no wonder I feel like this. I read it and it comes back vividly, the way I viewed life and how I interpreted what was happening. I might have buried a memory and forgotten it, but there it is.

Reflecting on Books

I like to read nonfiction, especially books that shed light upon who we are as a human species and where we're going. When I read a book that really moves me, *The Third Chimpanzee* by Jared M. Diamond, for example, I respond to it in my

From a visit to the U. S. Virgin Islands

journal. Diamond's book is about the origins of human life, looking at fossil records, figuring out when we first started speaking and where the first civilizations sprung up, why some evolved, why some people developed tools and why some didn't.

Outdoor Adventures

It seems obvious to me that the most inspiration for journal writing comes from going out into the natural world. Children aren't going to write or sketch in a journal if they're sitting in front of a television or computer screen. It doesn't matter where you go. You can get down and look at vegetation growing along the side of a city street or study a tree and all the creatures that inhabit it.

I don't think journal writing should be structured. For kids, the whole idea is for them to write about what they feel like writing. If they feel like writing poetry, great. Whatever is important to them is what goes in their journal. If they want to record what they're observing, such as pigeons mating or caterpillars in the grass of a vacant lot, fine. Basically, the journal is a vehicle for getting ideas, feelings, and observations on paper.

Journal as Friend

Growing up I had a group of neighborhood friends. We hung out together, but they didn't understand my love of nature. They didn't relate to it the way I did, and I often felt alone. There's always the child who marches to a different drummer. Writing in a journal is a way to share feelings, just like Anne Frank did in her diary. For the child without a close friend, the journal can be that friend.

Rich Wallace

"Dictated by Emotion"

Rich Wallace, age 6

Young adult novelist Rich Wallace survived late adolescence by running, listening to music, and writing in a diary. He says that a chart of his emotional life from age seventeen to twenty-one would resemble the printout of an EKG.

Almost daily, for four years, Wallace sorted out his life in 2-by-3-inch books: Would he win the next track meet? What did his future hold? He transcribed his fluctuating emotions into tiny printing and kept his journals hidden from his family, including the three older brothers against whom he measured himself. His self-imposed pressure to succeed with girls, on the track, and in life was intense, so Wallace needed a safety valve.

He hung with his buddies on street corners in Hasbrouck Heights, New Jersey—good friends, but reticent hometown boys. Instinctively, Wallace turned to writing.

Wallace needed to hear stories from other guys who had grappled with adolescent coming-of-age concerns. Folk rock musicians Jim Croce, Harry Chapin, Bob Dylan, and Bruce Springsteen, singers who were saying the things Wallace was feeling but couldn't yet express, spoke directly to him. He listened intently and transferred their lyrics to his journal.

Wallace identified with the messages of Springsteen, who mined small-town New Jersey landscapes and took his lyrics directly from what he saw around him: kids hanging on street corners, blue-collar workers trudging home from factories and yearning for a better life. Springsteen's music gave dignity to these lives. He understood their hopes and disappointments; his lyrics revealed respect and compassion for people just trying to make it through the day. All this spoke to Wallace because at seventeen, he was trying to define himself while searching for a way to become independent and take his place in the world.

Wallace's journals contain a four-year slice of life wedged between the typical, happy childhood that came before and the independence that followed: college, a nine-year career as sports writer, fatherhood, a career as editor and author. Growing up in a small town where athletics was one direct pathway to fame, Wallace participated in baseball, basketball, football, track, and cross country. He defined himself by competing on athletic fields. By age eighteen, Wallace knew he wanted to become a writer. In the back of his mind he recognized that someday his journals might be a useful resource.

When he began writing fiction, Wallace stopped keeping a journal. Writing fiction, he says, is the same kind of "purging and sorting out, but in a veiled way." To create settings and characters, Wallace draws on the inner landscape of adolescence as recorded in his diaries. Throughout *Wrestling Sturbridge*, Wallace's first young adult novel, the narrator tries to pin down a definition of himself in the short lists he writes at the beginning of each chapter—lists of his likes and dislikes, best and worst things about his town, places he wants to go and doesn't, questions he's not ready to answer. Ben's attempts at self-definition resemble Wallace's own high school efforts to tap a richer life, one beyond competitive sports.

> 2/20/76: "Things are cool. I'm psyched to go out tonite — with Herbie, Joey — haven't drank in a while/cool
> 5/1/76: "Cindy was here last nite. We fought—only a short one—but we both cried."

Venting anger and confusion in his journal brought Wallace relief. He admits never knowing where his life was going, day to day, sometimes hour to hour. What kept him writing so intensely, he says, "was being able to look back a week later and say 'Well, I got through that.'" Knowing that his down days didn't last very long and that he had a place to set aside sadness and frustration, Wallace rode out the emotional highs and lows of his teenage years. Now, looking back at those diaries, he finds them to be a valuable resource for his fiction.

While *Wrestling Sturbridge* and *Shots on Goal* are several steps removed from autobiography—he never wrestled or played soccer except recreationally—they mirror the turbulent, raw emotions of Wallace's life. Rereading his journals, Wallace races back in time, reliving events and the emotions attached to them. "Being able to remember a situation with my friends or a girl and really knowing how I felt, whether it was up or down, good or bad, that to me is the greatest benefit that the journals have provided."

Rich Wallace's books include

Wrestling Sturbridge
Shots on Goal

The Interview

I started keeping a diary when I was seventeen, and I wrote in it almost daily for about four years. My grandfather was an electrician in Kearny, New Jersey, and he used to give away small address books to his clients. They were two inches by three inches with a kind of fake leather cover on them and about thirty pages for entries. I took a supply of those from his house. I wrote in the tiniest handwriting I could possibly use, about the size of classified ad type, or box scores, as tiny as I could print. I crammed a lot onto one of those pages.

My family didn't know I was a journal keeper. I kept that absolutely hidden from the world. I hid my diary. I wouldn't let anybody near it. I didn't lock it, but I kept it where I didn't think anybody would stumble across it.

My whole life was changing. I was faced with these enormous pressures and frustrations, which in retrospect look trivial and like normal teenage stuff—getting some independence from home and struggling with what my future might be and who my girlfriend might be. I really needed to sort things out. I had a lot of friends, but we weren't exactly the most sensitive guys about each others' problems. So I started writing.

What I learned quickly, and what kept me writing so intensely, was being able to look back, even only a couple of weeks after an entry and say, "Well, I got through that. I'm still struggling, I'm still frustrated, I'm still really confused and sad about this stuff, but I got through it." I could look back and say, "I'm having another bad day right now, but my pattern is that the down days don't last very long."

Teenage Emotional Rollercoaster

When I started keeping a diary, I had a lot pent up that I didn't have any outlet for. I jumped into writing as a way of expressing my feelings. I had read John Lennon's journal. Even though it was really boring and monotonous—he wrote the same things day after day—I think that might be what spurred me to do it. I'd always written things, so it wasn't unusual for me to start making notes to myself.

At that point in my life I felt a real pressure to accomplish something, soon. I had three older brothers, who had probably gone through the same sorts of things I did. They had each succeeded in areas where I hadn't yet, particularly with girls. I wasn't facing any life or death issues, but I had just been dumped by my first girlfriend. In their peer groups, my brothers were probably a notch or two higher than I was and they had each exerted the kind of independence that I was just starting to gear up for.

It was simple things like losing a girlfriend or arguing with my parents, not doing very well in school or being frustrated over how I did in a race. To me these were life-shaping events. At the time I had three things that kept me kind of sane. One was the journal.

Another was listening to music. I have no musical ability whatsoever, but at the time I got into listening to folk rock musicians who wrote lyrics rather than just songs. They all wrote about the kinds of things I was going through, which was comforting. I needed to know that other people had gone through this and survived. One thing that shows up throughout the earliest diaries is lyrics from Jim Croce, Harry Chapin, and Bob Dylan. These guys were saying things that I wanted to say, but couldn't express myself. They affirmed that there were people who shared my frustrations.

The other thing was running. I was very much into track and field and defined myself as a runner. I was a junior in high school when I started writing a journal, with two years of competitive track and field behind me. With only my junior and senior seasons ahead of me, I realized that if I were going to be good, it had to be this season and the next season. Each of my brothers had been very successful in track and field, too, and I wanted at least to match them, if not outdo them. So I challenged myself in these diaries to succeed and to excel.

Writing helped me gain perspective on those things. Usually I didn't even try to reflect. I just wrote down what was going on and why I was angry or confused about it. Over time I would look back and say, well, now I can see how I worked that one out.

There were times when I wrote three or four entries a day and I would record what time of day I was writing. I can see enormous mood swings from 3 p.m. to 11 p.m. sometimes. I would have written something on Saturday afternoon and then gone out and come back later and either have been drunk or upset over something and there would have been big changes (usually upward) over those few hours. Today my emotional state is very much the same from minute to minute and from month to month, but when I look back at those journals it's like reading an electrocardiogram, up and down, up and down.

Journal as a Slice of Life

What's captured in those journals is a solid piece of my life fixed within a four-year period. When I was a teenager going through those years, they seemed liquid, a period of sorting things out, purging emotions. Now, looking back, I see a layer of my life pressed between the years that came before and after. It's a piece of my life, in and of itself, a layer I can mine for my fiction.

When I was eighteen I had some idea that what I was recording could be the basis for something later. I didn't keep my diary with that intent, but I think I was always aware that there was a resource there. In the first novel I wrote, unpublished, which was just one small step removed from autobiography, I drew on my journals pretty heavily. Even the kid who is telling the story is a journal keeper and in between each chapter is a diary entry, lifted almost word for word from my own. When going back to the diaries as a resource, I find they don't help in the least with plotting but they help with recalling scenes and characters and especially emotions. So they're a good resource for that.

Wrestling Sturbridge is several steps removed from my life, but still I was able to go back to my teenage years again. In looking back at those diaries I can recall pretty vividly a scene or an event that happened and the emotion that was attached to it. That is the most important thing, being able to remember a situation with my friends or a girl and really knowing how I felt, whether it was up or down, good or bad. That to me is the greatest benefit that the journals have provided.

Audience, Honesty, and Privacy

I lied once in my journal, and for a whole year it festered. Finally I confessed my lie in my journal. I've found that you have to be brutally honest with yourself, and if you can't be honest when you're writing for yourself, you're never going to be. Also, don't write for an audience. Just for yourself. And keep it private, especially if it's the kind of journal I kept. Once I showed a section to my girlfriend. I shared some things I had written about her family, which weren't very nice. She was struggling with family issues, and I felt that by showing her these pages I would be giving her support. Unfortunately, she didn't take it that way. Of course, I was looking at things superficially.

In *Wrestling Sturbridge*, Ben keeps lists about his life. He lists the worst things about his town: there's nothing to do, there's no way out, there's no end in sight. Then he lists the best things: the wrestling team, the cinder blocks, the smell of cows from his bedroom window during the spring thaw. He lists the things he likes to eat and the things he doesn't, the places he wants to go and the places he doesn't, the things he might be doing in a year and the things he definitely won't. I'm not sure at what age keeping a journal is advantageous. It's probably different for every kid. But I think any teenager would benefit from having a private outlet in which to face things head on.

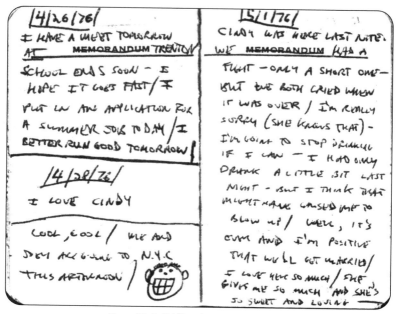

From Rich Wallace's teenage journal

Teenage Influences

If you were to look through my journals, you could see who my literary influences were, and they weren't Faulkner or Hemingway. They were people like Bob Dylan and Bruce Springsteen. More than the novelists, the people who influenced me the most were rock and rollers. My journals are filled with lyrics from the songwriters who were saying things I wanted to say, but couldn't say myself. I knew exactly what they meant when they sang of their frustrations and triumphs.

Springsteen was capturing snapshots of life in New Jersey, which is where I grew up. I was seventeen, living at night, hanging out on the Boulevard. The fact that somebody was singing about our experience elevated it and gave it dignity. We weren't just slobs hanging out on the corner, we were living lives. I had tremendous respect for my high school friends and still do. I know the picture that people driving by had of us, but I know what we really were all about. The fact that some songwriters were dignifying my life made me feel good. The people I write about in my books are the kids hanging out on the corners.

Letting Go

I stopped keeping a journal when I was married. It's not that I didn't have the time, I didn't have the emotional need. When I started to write fiction it took the place of diary writing. It's the same kind of purging and sorting out, but in a veiled way. Recently I tried to keep a journal again. For the first couple weeks I did it pretty regularly, but I ended every entry with "I'm not in sync with this yet, I don't know where I'm going with this, this doesn't feel right." I don't know why I even wanted to start again. I don't function the way I used to with those swings of emotions.

It felt like I was writing a newspaper column about my life. It was more "I did this and we did this and the weather was such and such." Maybe someday I'll get back to keeping a journal. Part of me misses it.

Terry Tempest Williams

"Embers from a Fire"

Terry Tempest Williams

Greatly influenced by her Mormon culture, which has a strong tradition of pioneer and western women journal keepers, nature writer Terry Tempest Williams began keeping a diary when she was seven years old. As a child, journal writing was a natural extension of her love for language and stories. In a little white diary with a lock and key, Williams established a sanctuary to hold her perceptions of life and unearthed a place to explore the world on the page. Today, journal keeping is so much a part of the fabric of her days that she is barely aware of it.

"Journal writing is the one thing in my life that I truly rely on for gravity and stability of soul," she says. Writing in her journal also reflects the rhythms and cycles of her life: when she's busy, weeks rush by with no attention given to daily notations. Williams writes more in winter when she is at home in Salt Lake City, for example, than she does in the spring and fall when she is working in the field. Traveling, she says, brings its own "built-in mechanism for space and solitude."

Williams notes how journal writing, as a practice and discipline, mirrors the personality of the individual. "I think of two friends, both men. One with whom I've been in the field keeps a journal every day. The other has had three journals in the past five years." For children, journal writing celebrates their spirits because it is playing on the page. It validates their voices. There are no rules. It's about freedom. A teacher for four years, Williams found journal writing the single most important gift she could give her students. "It was their time to really listen to themselves; it was when the noise stopped and thinking began."

Some people, she finds, are intimidated by the empty page; others fear beautiful, hand-made books. Just before her brother left for Africa, Williams presented him with a brown leather-bound journal, small enough to fit in the back pocket of his jeans. She encouraged him to carry it with him, especially when he ventured into the game parks. "Then you'll have lots of stories," she told him.

At breakfast, upon his return, her brother pulled out his journal. It was blank. Then he spread on the table sheets of scribbled paper. "I didn't write in this journal," he confessed. "It was so pretty I didn't want to wreck it, but I want you to know that I wrote on these pages, and now I'm going to transcribe them."

Appraising her shelf of journals from the past year, Williams finds many black, hardbound sketchbooks with spiral notebooks sprinkled in between. Arranged in no particular order, they illustrate the manic nature of those previous months. When she observes the row of journals written when her mother was very ill, the "Refuge" journals, she is struck by their uniformity. "That uniformity was the only thing I could count on. There was so much external chaos that I was forced to be much more disciplined internally. When my life is calm inside, I have much more leeway to play."

In the field, Williams records the natural world in sketch-like, impressionistic gestures. "I'm terrible at drawing," she says, "but the impulse behind the naturalist who sketches and my recording with images and metaphors is the same. I'm there, connected to the source."

In its aura of immediacy, her early children's book, *The Secret Language of Snow*, which explains snow's role in nature and its effects on animals and plant life, reveals Williams's ability to paint the natural world in words. In metaphor and image, she gathers the impressions that will kindle her imagination and fuel her professional writing. When Terry Tempest Williams refers to her field journals, she discovers one image that might evoke an entire landscape. "They're almost embers from a fire. I can blow right back into them and begin to see the entire scene."

Terry Tempest Williams's books include

The Secret Language of Snow, with Ted Major
Between Cattails
Refuge: An Unnatural History of Family and Place
An Unspoken Hunger: Stories from the Field
Pieces of White Shell: A Journey to Navajo Land
Desert Quartet

The Interview

In my family, because I was the only girl, my journal was a sanctuary. From the time I was seven or eight years old it became a place of privacy, a place where I could explore the world on the page. I remember a white diary, one that had a lock and a key, and that was very serious. What the lock said to me was that in these pages there was a loyalty I could always depend on. Privacy was never an issue. My mother preferred having me close the door to my bedroom, probably because my room was such a mess. The privacy of my diary was symbolic: this was a place I could entrust myself to.

River of Life

Journal keeping is an ongoing, continual process, the meandering of my day and the river of my creativity. The vehicle is always the pen, the page, and the river. There are times in my journal when I'm in an eddy, going around and around and around. There are other times where I'm engaged in white water and can feel myself going down a certain tongue of the river. Other times, I'm in flat water, where it's very peaceful.

When I travel I carry with me a special travel journal. I take a beautiful journal because it becomes an artifact. For example, when I went to Japan, I took a turquoise, leather-bound jour-

From the journal of Terry Tempest Williams

nal. It seemed very Japanese and honored the place where I was going. My travel journals are much more elaborate than my daily journals.

At home I use black sketchbooks, large ones so I have more room to write. In there goes everything from the meanderings of the day and daily perceptions to lecture notes, reading notes, photographs, leaves, and petals. When I'm in the field I carry pocket-sized spiral notebooks for descriptions and impressions. The difference between my black books and the field notebooks is the difference between essays and poems. I also keep day-books, which consist of lists, first drafts, and notes from conversations. For me the journal conveys the dance that we are engaged in, and that includes both the shadow and light of our days.

As for pens, I usually just use black felt tips. A friend of mine who is a conservator at the Utah Museum of Natural History in Salt Lake City, where I work, says they're going to self destruct in about ten years, they're all going to disappear. I suppose from the archival point of view we should all be using ballpoint pens.

Private Perceptions, Personal Prose

My journals are extremely private, my raw state of discovery. I go to my journal to explore my world on the page and to make sense of what I'm feeling. Since there may be references to other people or to conversations, things not to be talked about in a public way, I often write in a kind of shorthand. My audience is my own exploration. Writing in my journal is having a conversation across the table with someone I absolutely trust. It's the place where I am listened to.

When I write in my journal I'm not in the service of craft, not in that writer's trance, whereas when I'm working with art I'm in the service of the metaphoric and there is something moving through me. When I write a manuscript for publication, I take that which is private and work it through the lens

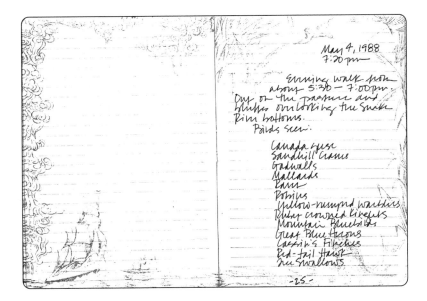

of craft and language so that it becomes both personal and universal.

Refuge: An Unnatural History of Family and Place came from twenty-three journals and yet, if you had asked me at the time if I were writing that book, I would have told you no. Whole passages from my journals do appear in *Refuge,* but what's different is that they are shaped into context. What I noticed while writing *Refuge* was that my public prose is much more personal than my journals.

Field Notes

I love field journals because they're sketchbooks, snapshots of imagery. I'm terrible at drawing, but the impulse behind the naturalist who sketches and my recording with images and metaphors is the same. I'm there, connected to the source. There's an energetic response in those journals that I can't retrieve from memory. They read almost like poetry in their immediacy of image and emotion.

As I go back and transcribe my journals, I'll find one word

that evokes an entire landscape for me, so I know exactly where I am. They're almost embers from a fire. I can blow right back into them and begin to see the entire scene.

When I'm writing an essay I'll take out my field notes and use the impressions for the structure. I'll do research, which adds the informative strands, and then create the narrative that weaves it all together. My journals hold the images.

Silent Generations

My mother and grandmothers never kept journals because they were so private they could never bear the thought that someday, someone would know what they had thought. My mother left me all her journals, and as a joke before she died she said, "Terry I want to leave you all of my journals." I thought, oh, how extraordinary, there's this part of my mother's life that I didn't know. She showed me where they were on the shelf and I opened them and they were all empty. I think the intention was there, but her sense of privacy was too ferocious.

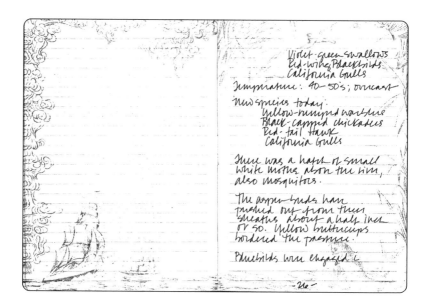

Too Busy Living Life

When my niece Callie turned twelve I took her to New York, as I do each of my nieces. We bought a special journal but she didn't keep it at all. I've noticed from my nieces that there's a fine line between experiencing life and recording life. They are so engaged in living their lives that they are not interested in sitting down and writing about them. One of the things that I have done with my nieces, which has been very fun, is to keep a notebook when we go into the field as a family. Children love to make lists, and we'll keep lists of the birds and animals we see. Then we'll add other elements—where we saw the birds, what was their niche, or their neighborhood, or their habitat. They become aware of the importance of keeping records. We keep these journals at my father's place in Wyoming and it's always fun to go back and see what we did the previous year. We begin to see the continuity of a place and also when things shift and change.

Bruce Coville

"Fishing for Memories"

Bruce Coville

"To be a writer," says Bruce Coville, "you have to have enough self-confidence, self-assurance, or arrogance, depending on how people define it, to think that what you have to say is worth reading. Otherwise, how can you justify expecting people to spend their time with your words? Taking it to the extreme, I have to think that some day somebody will want to read my journals as source material for the major tome they write on my life."

For Coville, who frequently uses his journals to sift through the emotional material of his intense life, such thinking creates a dilemma. "The more well-known I get, the more I feel myself inhibited about writing in my journal because the more sense I have that there might some day be another eye on it."

Torn between the importance of historical record and thinking it's nobody's business, Coville no longer feels as comfortable writing in his journal as he used to. At first he was shocked to learn that the papers of the explorer Richard Burton were burned by his wife after his death. "It's not unusual to read about a wife or one's family burning private papers. Sometimes I think that's appalling. Then I think, well I don't know if I want anybody reading my journals." While his papers, including all drafts for each new book are sent to the de Grummond Children's Literature Research Collection at the University of Southern Mississippi, his journals remain stashed in file cabinets, held strictly private. "They might get them when I'm dead, but they're not getting them now."

Writing with a future biographer and adoring public perched on his shoulder — Coville receives thousands of letters per year from his readers — is only one constraint on his journal keeping. The other is his fast-paced life. When he hasn't had to time to keep a journal, Coville misses the act of recording life. With a prolific career as a writer of juvenile fiction, musical plays, and fantasy stories and all the demands on his time — speaking engagements, school visits, interview requests — he finds life sometimes swirling "out of control." While Coville would love to capture in detail all the events of his extremely rich and textured life, he settles for shortcuts. He saves copies of computer correspondence, which he prints out at the end of the year and stuffs into manila envelopes and file folders. Rules don't apply. Should's, have to's and got to's just slow him down. Anything goes: notes scribbled on the back of an envelope and physical objects, like ticket stubs from a movie.

Some time ago Coville read in a writers' magazine that keeping a journal was a good idea. Thirty years and thousands of pages later, he still thinks it such a good idea that he encourages children who want to be writers to keep a journal. "The human brain is cranky. If you want an idea, your mind will probably refuse to give it to you. Sometimes ideas just come floating by. The trick is to save ideas when they come to you. If you get a great idea today, it will probably be gone before you get around to writing about it — unless you write it down."

Born in Syracuse, New York, Coville grew up near his grandparents' dairy farm, three miles outside the small town of Phoenix in central New York. As a child he arose before everyone else in the family so he could cuddle in a chair and read *The Voyages of Dr. Dolittle.* What some people consider junk was a staple in his childhood reading diet: Nancy Drew, the Hardy Boys, and zillions of comic books. His only regret is the time he spent watching television when he could have been reading instead. When his grandparents visited Florida, Coville would write them long letters describing family happenings. He would make a carbon and put it into a journal, keeping a record of what had happened during the week.

The first time he can remember thinking that he would like to become a writer came in the sixth grade, when his teacher, Mrs. Crandall, gave the class an extended period of time to write a long story. He was smitten. At age seventeen he began working seriously at writing. By age nineteen he knew he wanted to write fiction for children. Unable to sell his stories right away, he worked many other jobs including toy maker, gravedigger, cookware salesman, and assembly-line worker. Eventually he became an elementary teacher and worked with second and fourth graders.

For children who want to write, for anyone who wants to write, Coville offers a few tips: "Talent is only part of what it takes to be a writer. Luck, courage and mostly just plain old sticking to it are just as important. Never give up. You must believe in yourself, even when no one else does. Read a lot. Filling your brain with good stuff is an important part of the job. Write a lot. Keep a journal," he concludes. "It's one of the best tools a writer has."

Bruce Coville's books include

Aliens Stole My Body and other Bruce Coville Alien Adventures
My Teacher Glows in the Dark
Jeremy Thatcher, Dragon Hatcher
Dragonslayers
Bruce Coville's Book of Ghosts
Into the Land of Unicorns

The Interview

I started keeping a journal in college. I probably read in some writers' magazine that it was a good idea and I tried to do everything that I read about writing. I tried to do everything that was supposed to be a good idea, and that was one of the things that was supposed to be a good idea. The college journal was an on-again, off-again thing, but I have extensive journals for the last twenty years.

Cranky Files

I have had an intense personal life, and one of the purposes of the journal was to write through that stuff. Having avoided the mid-life crisis by quitting my job and deciding to do what I wanted with my life when I was thirty, I have been through most of that *tsuris*, at least for the time being. Now my life is more settled — theoretically that's one of the things that happens as you get older — so I don't write as much because I'm not as upset. A time of crisis will prompt me to get it out and use it. For example, I write when I get cranky; I have separate "cranky files." The cranky file is a way of mending stuff and a way of working through things, getting it out of my system, so instead of exploding I can talk to people in a rational way. And sometimes saying, "Oh, well this wasn't such a bad thing they did."

Journal Files

I also write about what's going on in my life. I don't have a bound journal. What I do is type my journal at the computer. Even before I had a computer I typed my journal. And so I've simply kept it in a manila envelope marked 1981, 1994, 1995. I have a file drawer full of manila folders from 1975 to the present. With the typed journal pages, which I use as a way of remembering things, or even putting in for my future biographer, I've tossed in carbons of letters. When my grandparents were alive and would go to Florida I would write long letters to them about what was going on with the family, and I would make a carbon and put it in the journal because it kept a record of what had happened that week.

Right now my life is out of control and I am less active about journal keeping. I miss having the record of my life. My life is extremely rich and extremely fast-paced right now, and I would like to save more of it than I do.

Savings Account

One way I save things, by the way, is on a computer network. I exchange messages with people on there every day and I download the file and save it, and it functions to some extent as a journal. These casual written conversations have a journalistic function because usually I talk about what I'm doing on a given day. I stuff those into my journal files.

I have a file on my computer where I list the books I read in a given year, the movies I see, the plays I go to. For the movies I write down who I went with, where the play was done. I have another file marked "pages," which is where I keep track of the writing I do for each project. I print all those out at the end of the year and stuff those in the journal, too.

Fishing for Memories

Our life is imprinted on our brain, but we can't pull it all up.

The journal is like a fishhook you can drop in your brain and pull out memories very efficiently. The sights and sounds and the smells are going to come rushing back to you. Some of the journal entries I like best go back to when my kids were little. Did I say twenty years? Actually my journal goes back twenty-five years. Somewhere between twenty and twenty-five years. I used to write a lot about what the kids did when they were little.

Actually, one of my first nonfiction articles grew out of that record. I wrote an article for *Sesame Street Newsletter* called "A Father's Journal" about these things that were saved in that journal. These funny things the kids did would be lost if they hadn't been written down there. Occasionally I would just be looking through it and I would go and tell my wife something the kids had done and she would say, "How did you remember that? I'd completely forgotten about that." It was all written down there. My daughter, who is now in her twenties, will say, "Tell me something funny I did when I was a little kid." She loves to know about when she was little. She was born in 1975, and I can pull out my journal from 1977, which is about three or four hundred pages long, and there are wacko little kid things that she did recorded in there. I can go back and pull out stories about when she was killing bugs with her mother's toothbrush.

Fish Bait

I tell kids that there are a number of ugly truths about their lives, and one of them is that everything fades. If I'm with a group of fifth graders I'll say, "There's probably not one of you here who can tell me in detail what happened your first day of first grade, a very important day in your life, but it's all recorded in your under brain. It's all registered there, and there is a way to save it and that's by keeping a journal. Journal keeping is a way of saving your life, saving yourself for yourself, a gift you give yourself, a gift you give yourself ten years later." I tell them about keeping a journal and using it like a fishhook to pull up images. I tell them that when I read a sentence in my journal it can bring up a whole day in my mind.

Don't think in terms of have to, or gotta, or this is the right way and this is the wrong way. There is not a wrong way to keep a journal. I think throwing in ticket stubs is a perfectly valid thing to do in a journal. Ten years later you fish out ticket stubs for the junior prom or a movie you went to. That's a memory. The journal can be not only things you write but physical objects you stick in there and save. It can be written on the back of envelopes that you stick in the folder. What slowed me down in the past was thinking I should do this or I should do that. There's no should or got to with a journal; it's what's useful for you.

Not Just for Writers

One of the things a writer has to do is practice, and keeping a journal is good practice in the same way that playing backyard basketball will help you if you're going to grow up to be a basketball player. The other thing is that a writer's primary source material is the self, and by keeping the journal they preserve that source. But I hate to see journal keeping restricted to writers. I hate it when I go to a school and a principal introduces me and says, "Today you are going to meet a real writer." Take away the principal and these kids are already real writers, or they should be. Writing is a skill that is the most human of all skills, the one that differentiates us as a species. Exercising written language is the most human thing a person can do.

Keeping a journal is a great thing for a writer, but self awareness is something that all human beings should be deeply immersed in trying to achieve. Journal keeping is a significant tool for anybody who is breathing and has a brain.

Patricia Lee Gauch

"Can You Hear My Voice?"

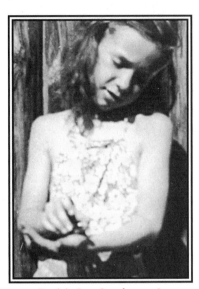

Patricia Lee Gauch, age 9,
holding a turtle

As author, editor, and vice president and editorial director at Philomel Books, Patricia Lee Gauch finds little time there days for writing in her journal. Life is too hectic, her schedule too erratic. But on vacation, in the quiet of late afternoon, Gauch retreats to her journal to "savor as well as save" the exquisite moments of the day. When she's had an adventure, she can hardly wait to set down the details of the experience in words.

Gauch first befriended her journal in the eleventh grade when her English teacher introduced the concept of keeping a journal. Looking back, she recognizes how this assignment to connect personal reflections with feelings and incidents in the literature seemed, in the 1950s, way ahead of its time. After college, Gauch explored her environment as a reporter for the *Louisville Courier-Journal* in Louisville, Kentucky. With energy and zest, she listened to people's stories and captured details in a reporter's notebook. In her next career, as writer and editor of children's literature, Gauch created successful picture books as well as young adult novels. Known for her Christina Katerina and Tanya stories, among others, she has explored those personal and family problems commonly experienced by young girls.

In novels like *The Green of Me, Kate Alone,* and *The Year the Summer Died,* Gauch dramatizes the emotional world of late-teen girls who face boyfriend issues, family responsibility, and peer group complexities. Touchstone of her creative work is considerable skill at inventing high-spirited main characters. Gauch has also garnered praise for the rhythms of her writing and for the way her dialogue captures the immediacy of scenes.

As an editor, Gauch is interested in that elusive quality known as voice. However it's defined — energy, spirit, essence, breath, or voice — in character or narration, every story has to have it. According to Gauch, voice "follows the rhythms of your own body — your breathing, your personality, how excitable you are, how laid back you are." Since each character and every book has some part of the author in it, this will be reflected in voice. The journal is the writer's workplace where voice breathes, whispers, stutters, sputters, and bellows. Writing in a journal is entering a secret garden where no one else ventures. It's good for discovering and using voice. Nothing is at stake. No one is offering advice. It is the place for letting go, which is where, Gauch finds, most good writing comes from.

Gauch says she does not use her journal as a direct source for fiction. Instead she writes there to recapture experience and to explore the sensory details of this marvelous world. "Writing in a journal can be a way to capture a peak moment — to live it twice and thrice." Then, as she plays with words to record tastes, sights, sounds, and feelings, Gauch hones her craft by striving to get close to the bone, to touch emotions and truth, and to create authenticity in her writing.

> Summer, 1993. Haworth, England: I have wanted to see Haworth for a long time. Every time I taught *Wuthering Heights* I walked into the very houses, across the very moors of Cathy and Heathcliff. Now that I think of it, his home says it all, doesn't it? He was both green and warm with growth, and hard, impenetrable. Moody, but not at first. His environment did that to him. (Wasn't Darwin publishing in 1848; interesting that his theories and Emily's coincide.) The town of Haworth is a harsh little town, soot-black from industry clinging to Penistone Hill. The Black Bull Inn (where the brother drank himself to death) must only be 100 yards from Patrick Bronte's church (rebuilt) and behind that the heath leading to the open moors. John [my son] and I walked to the waterfall. So must the four of them. They were so frail in the end. Not of the moors; somehow of a pampered—or at least protected—civilization. The girls all Cathy: romantic spirited but in their way.

Finding the wisdom of one's life and then returning it to children through literature is Gauch's quest as an author and editor. At the 1996 Highlights Foundation Writers Workshop at Chautauqua, Gauch exhorted writers to write from the heart with spirit and confidence: Find the story in yourself. Let ideas come from what impassions, what embarrasses, excites, infuriates. Know this world well, for most fiction is rooted in detail. Free yourself to hear your own voice and your character's voice, down to the hums and ahas. Go deep and wide and explore all the possibilities of life. Then, sing out loud so children gain a sense of what's possible and learn to exercise their own voices.

Patricia Lee Gauch's books include

Noah
Christina Katerina and the Box
Tanya and Emily in a Dance for Two

This Time, Tempe Wick?
Thunder at Gettysburg
Aaron and the Green Mountain Boys

The Interview

When I was in the eleventh grade I had an English teacher who was way ahead of his time. He had us keep reading journals. It was back in the fifties, and it was not done frequently then. We got quite personal in our reflections, using the journal to connect personal reflections and feelings with incidents in the literature.

Today I keep journals at exquisite moments, when I've had an experience that I want to savor as well as save. My journal is a place to remember the epiphanies of my life, to explore the sensory detail of this wonderful world, to spirit words and discern the source of ideas.

Last year my husband and I took six weeks in New Zealand. I savored each adventure: rafting the Clutha River with a guide, seeing an albatross glide, discovering a seal colony. I could hardly wait at the end of the day to sit down with my journal. It's like chatting with a friend, going over it all again. I savored each moment as I tried to recapture the experience at the end of the day. Writing in a journal can be a way to capture a peak moment—to live it twice and thrice. Lucky me that it was there again when I read my journal upon my return.

A major part of writing is trying to create an authentic piece of work. You get close to the bone with your writing when you touch emotions or experiences that you had in your own life. In my journal I'm playing with words to recover experience— taste, touch, sight and feelings—and at the same time I'm honing my craft. I'm going for an emotional hit, for verisimilitude.

Finding Your Voice

One of the major searches in a writer's life is for voice. The journal is so good for developing voice because journal writing is conversational. It's attempting to catch the rhythms of your own body, it's uneven, it's aberrant, and I think that's voice. It follows the rhythms of your own body—your breathing, your personality, how excitable you are, how laid back you are. Voice is a profile of your body, a thumbprint of it. The journal is one of the best places to practice finding voice because nothing is at stake.

The journal is a wonderful place to explore the turning points in one's life, which is generally what a person selects when writing a personal essay. It's the natural voice and the conversational feeling, as if you are telling a story to someone. It's the most intimate someone because it is yourself. You're not proving and you're not selling anything. All you know is that there is a story you would like to tell. You explore something. Then there's the summation, the wisdom that comes out of whatever it is that happens to you.

Advice for Writers

Most good writing comes from letting go. The journal gives people a private place to explore and be alone. You travel through gates into a secret garden where nobody else is welcome. Because of the requirements of state and city and country there are a lot of rules and regulations for kids when they're writing. The journal is a wonderful opportunity to discover the true writer in oneself, an opportunity to let go, to search for voice, to search for stories without anyone interfering or offering advice. It certainly goes to the subconscious much more easily than most assignments do and, of course, that is where the richness of being a writer is.

Naomi Shihab Nye

"A Constellation of Images"

Naomi Shihab Nye, age 5

There was no moment of decision when Naomi Shihab Nye announced, "I am going to keep a notebook." Her first journals were the ones she made in second grade — large sheets of paper sewn together with embroidery thread. Teacher Harriett B. Lane of St. Louis, a strong advocate of poetry, taught her students to copy poems into their notebooks so they could learn new words and see how lines were constructed.

By copying the poems of great poets, Nye says, "I began to learn the pleasures of gathering voices on paper." She also started writing poems of her own and mailing them to children's magazines. She knew that if she were going to be a writer, she would have to write on a frequent, consistent, and comfortable basis. Journals of all shapes and sizes became her constant companions. In high school Nye wrote in a journal to try to keep her composure in the midst of swirling passions and disappointments. She wondered how people who didn't keep journals were able to survive.

Nye keeps many journals simultaneously and her mood determines which one she picks up. She doesn't always date the entries. She writes on scraps of paper and later tucks or tapes them inside. She doesn't worry about who might see it, now or in the future, since one would have to be a Sherlock Holmes to piece together her life from her journals.

Students often ask Nye where she gets her ideas. "Where do I not get ideas?" she replies. Copying signs has always been a quick way for her to capture the essence of a place. For her poem "Lost," Nye roamed her neighborhood jotting down lost animal notices. Her son Madison is also a source of ideas, and Nye keeps separate journals of his quotations.

> Madison: "People at this airport like to say 'approximately' a lot."
> Madison on phone in Alaska to Sidi and Nana (his grandparents, back home in Texas): "We ate king crabs. Each one was as big as 2 telephones."

Nye's picture book *Benito's Dream Bottle* is based on a story Madison used to tell when he was two and three. Nye encourages children to be very generous in what they write down. The journal is the place to be lavish, to collect gems and tidbits. In her travel journals, early morning journals of random writing, conversation journals filled with lines overheard, and observation journals, Nye says she gets down more than she will ever use. "The journal helps us remember the motto: the more we write, the more we have to write."

Naomi Shihab Nye's books include

Sitti's Secrets
Benito's Dream Bottle
Lullaby Raft
Never in a Hurry: Essays on People and Places
Fuel (poems)
Habibi

The Interview

My second-grade teacher, Harriett B. Lane of St. Louis, was a strong poetry advocate. How lucky we were to have her. She believed everything her students needed was contained in poetry—vocabulary, punctuation, imagery, history, hope—everything. She would impress upon us the importance of copying other people's lines into our notebooks so we could see how the lines were constructed and so we could learn new words. She also encouraged memorization and reading aloud. My first journals were the ones I made in her class where she taught us to sew pages together with big needles and heavy embroidery thread. These books were huge, the size of large sheets of construction paper, because second graders have such big printing. We would copy other people's poems in them—Dickinson, Sandburg, Blake. And we would write original poems and original lines in them, too. She also encouraged us to copy poems written by our fellow classmates. These writings were central texts of second grade. I began to learn the pleasures of gathering voices on paper.

Personal Growth

As a high school student I remember thinking I might be a maniac if I couldn't write in my journal. It saved me. It let me stand back and look at my swirling life with a bit of composure, anyway. I wrote about all my melodramatic teenage experiences, all the passions and disappointments, and wondered how people who didn't do this could even survive.

In college we were asked to keep dream journals for a psychology course. The idea was that every person has a constellation of images that appear in the mind—the unconscious and in dreams—and that it is helpful to become conversant with this set of images. By keeping a dream journal one could become aware of patterns and the images one used to describe or embody experience. I seemed to dream often of sofas or couches, for example, something I never think of in waking life! What I learned was that the more I wrote from my dreams, the more I remembered my dreams.

I don't write them all down these days, but often wake with clear direction from or impressions of them. As we grow older and more balanced, more comfortable with our emotional experiences, ha ha, the uses for the personal journal shift and change. Now I think everything is a dream. Or it's all mixed together.

Creative Disorganization

I don't keep just one journal, but many simultaneously. I am not a meticulous journal keeper; I don't always date things. Actually, I'm a mess. Sometimes I start writing on little scraps of paper and tape or tuck them into a journal. You couldn't go through any of my journals chronologically because they jump around a lot and my mood determines which one I pick up to write in. Sometimes I have to be a detective to find what I need. Maybe general disorganization is a part of my creative process. My journals are a mixture and I want them to be. I am a mixture. My brain is a mixture, so my journals would have to be. I wouldn't want one kind of journal. That would be lying.

I always have kept separate conversation journals where I record, as an eavesdropper or as a secretary, things that other people say, quotes, conversations, overheard lines. I've always kept travel journals that are specific to a trip or a stay some-where. I've kept various notebooks containing quotes from our son. The years two and three were particularly replete with wondrous language. These have helped later in stories and poems. Then there are the random journals, early-morning writing wandering widely. I might draw little squiggly lines in between things, but drawing is not a large part of my journal keeping. I paste in quotes or poems or headlines that seem intriguing and worth thinking about.

Lost-Pet Posters

Copying signs has always been an essential part of my jour-nal keeping. In my travel journal from a trip to India I drew what the signs looked like and copied the words. One said "Baby Boom is Nation's Doom!" Signs are a quick way to cap-ture the flavor of a place.

I grew up in St. Louis, an old city full of decaying, strange signs. One that I copied down as a child was from a dilapidat-ed shack in our neighborhood that said in faded orange letters, "Serving the hotdog with dignity." I remember writing it down and thinking, "Well, what is a hotdog with dignity? Did it mean that the server had dignity? Or the dog itself?" It's one of those details that would have disappeared if I hadn't written it down. Later, when I was grown, it became part of a poem.

A sign on a shack near Waco, Texas: "TNT Barbecue—Terrible Delicious." I guess they meant Terribly Delicious. I love the Bug Scuffle Ranch, a name copied near Vanderpool, Texas, and the Welcome to Onionville signs by Texarkana.

For my poem "Lost," which is about lost pet posters, I went around my neighborhood for months copying lost animal notices. One I found after writing the poem said in a child's crooked handwriting, "Please help us look for our dog Asia. She is orange and very large. She has never known anything but kindness."

Adding to the Confusion

Notebooks that cost fifty cents at the grocery store are quite sufficient. Some people like fancier hardbound books. The notebooks I've always favored are gray Jerusalem copy books with Arabic on the outside. When I lived in Jerusalem as a teenager these were the copy books we did our homework in. They're very flexible and small, maybe eight inches by six inches, so I can fold them in half and stick them into a pocket or a purse. I never noticed until someone commented on it, but I often write in them from back to front, as Arabic goes, because the place for one's name is on the back. Even though I'm writing in English, writing back to front adds to my general chaos. Sometimes it may help me spring loose in some way. It feels good to subvert our own systems now and then.

> April 7 - enroute to Dutch
> Harbor / Unalaska, Aleutian
> Islands —
>
> Madison. "People at the airport
> like to say "approximately"
> a lot."
>
> We stayed last night at
> the dignified, dark-interiored
> Hotel Captain Cook in
> Anchorage. Michael had flown
> on a day ahead of us: although
> we hear today that our flight
> has 10 seats remaining open,
> they wouldn't let him have
> one with his flight coupon.
> So he flew on ahead + got
> rerouted onto a smaller
> craft. His call upon arrival
> confirmed the wide
> reputation of landings in

From Naomi Shihab Nye's journal

I have crates and crates of journals, some of which are stored in the attic in old suitcases, which I buy at the Salvation Army and garage sales for two dollars. Some of my journals are in a filing cabinet in our garage. Really, they're all over. I have twelve around me right now and stacked up on a nearby shelf are twenty-five to thirty from the last ten years.

Wispy Fragments and Snatches of Things

One thing I notice about poets vs. the journal-keeping fiction writers I know is that poets seem to be a lot more satisfied with little bits of things that don't have any threads tying them together. Poets don't need a lot to get them going. Fiction writers will keep putting down notes about the character, the setting, the story. Poets don't need plots or sequences. Poets can just stare if they feel like it. Poets tend to write wispy fragments and feel good about it. I don't experience any resistance about writing down snatches of things. Even a journal without a single complete sentence would be a good journal to me.

Drawing on the Details

I never assume that anything I write in my notebook is going to be worked into something larger. It would be unrealistic and it would pressure me into thinking that every entry is crucial. I try to cultivate a relaxed alertness that picks up bits and pieces that I may or may not use. I want the possibility of not "using" the majority of the gathered wealth! Although my current motto is "use what you have," that's just to remind me we have aplenty at all times. About three or four times a year I stack up a bunch of notebooks on my table and start poking into them and pulling things out. I'm drawing on things that haven't connected before or been developed. Often I come up with new images of scenes this way. It's very mysterious which notebooks rise to the surface. A few years ago I took out my India journal and ended up writing an essay about a trip that had occurred ten years earlier. If I hadn't had the journal about that particular segment of our trip, which contains crucial details, names, distances, bird facts, etc., I wouldn't have been able to write the essay. Although I was writing from a new perspective of distance, all those particulars kept me from writing in a vacuum.

I wrote notes about my Palestinian grandmother for years—she died three years ago at the age of 106. Some of those notes worked their way into my children's book *Sitti's Secrets* and numerous poems and essays.

By Invitation Only

I'm flamboyantly open when I write in my notebook and I don't worry about anyone seeing it who shouldn't see it or about someone in the future getting ahold of it. I operate on old-fashioned respect: you do what you want in your journal because you know no one will read it unless they've been invited. I've always lived in a household that embodied respect, both with my parents and with my husband and son, and we don't go around reading each other's things unless encouraged to.

My husband keeps very interesting journals, which document his experiences as a photographer. He doesn't ever have to worry about privacy issues, though, because his handwriting is completely illegible.

Advice for Young Writers

I encourage children to be very, very generous with what they write, getting down lots more than they will ever use. Many of them have been told lately (and I find this very dubious advice) that they should finish everything they start. No way! What a burden that is for a notebook. If they can't think of anything to write, I encourage them to start with a question. What three things would I like to remember about today? What do I care about that I haven't shared with anyone today? What worries me right now? Children should not feel compelled to

keep a close record on their movements, in the old diary format—what I ate, what the weather was like, etc. This starts
feeling too tedious too quickly. The journal is the place to be
lavish and free in expression, the place to collect gems and tidbits that the child can go back to later.

For a few years I was obsessed with the observation walk. I
would take students for walks in their neighborhoods. They
would have to be completely silent and write down things that
they noticed. When we came back to the classroom, people
would share their lists. It was always interesting to compare
what people noticed—something crucial or striking to one person hadn't been observed at all by others, or perhaps three students described a person at the bus stop in three different ways.
I was giving them the idea that a notebook is a stimulant. From
now on they could be a little more awake and alive, noticing
their surroundings and collecting bits and pieces for future
writing.

One thing that's true about writing: the more we write, the
more we have to write. Journals help us remember that motto.
The act of writing gives us lots more material, more details,
more characters, more conversations, than we ever had to begin
with.

Settle Down

The two most useful things any writer can do is read widely
and keep notebooks, writing on a regular basis. William
Stafford, my favorite poet, believed that we must train ourselves to become more alert and attentive to all the messages,
signs, and images around us, and that keeping an ongoing, regular notebook was one of the best exercises for maintaining
alertness. A notebook affords us time: we don't have to feel the
urgency to compose things right away. All that's necessary at
first is to get down skeletal bits, images, and impressions. The
thing that often works against adults is preoccupation. We feel
like we have to be in twelve places at one time. That doesn't

make for comfortable writing. Notebooks help us settle down and focus. No one is going to give us the time; we have to make it.

A Place of Collection

Years ago I read someone describe the journal as that drawer in the kitchen where you pitch all the birthday candles and coupons and recipes that you haven't used yet. I think of my notebook as that drawer with all the weird stuff that doesn't go together, a useful jumble. I also think of it as a secret room, a room in which I have odd objects that I don't have to defend. In this secret room I put the fossil I found on a walk or the strange spoon that suddenly appeared in a drawer. The letter from a beloved friend. The scrap of Japanese paper. I go in there and move things around. When I'm writing, I'm moving around objects in my secret room.

For a speech I was scheduled to give in Japan, I invented the title before I wrote the talk, titling it *Wind in a Bucket*. I wrote it in a notebook and sent it to them for their program. Then I had to come up with remarks that would fit. I had the title but I was still writing the talk when I arrived. I bought a beautiful Japanese bucket and walked along on the beach collecting odd little things like snippets of ribbons, or a shell or a stump of a pencil. There wasn't much litter in Japan so I had to pay close attention indeed! I think of my notebook as this bucket: a place of collection.

Kim Stafford

"Faith in a Fragment"

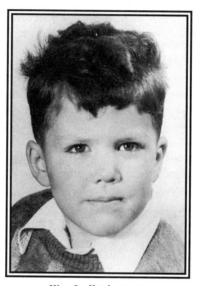

Kim Stafford, age 4

Tucked into his shirt pocket, along with a pen, is a palm-sized, hand-sewn journal. Kim Stafford reaches for his "heart pocket book" to harvest a conversation overheard, an idea bubbling up, serendipitous poetic discoveries. Director of the Northwest Writing Institute at Lewis and Clark College in Portland, Oregon, Stafford rushes about meeting his obligations to academe. To this busy father with a new baby, stretches of solitude are few. Because he keeps his journal handy, he can take any moment to scribble notes to be held for later reflection. On the telephone, while waiting at the bus stop, or sitting through committee meetings, Stafford nets material from the abundance of everyday life. His pocket journal permits him close attention to the world around him. He trusts that what he records, however fragmented or fleeting, will nurture future writing projects.

Fundamentally, all of Stafford's writing is born in his journal. He accumulates about a dozen heart pocket books a year and annually gathers them into bundles bound with string. Each little brick, he says, feels like a treasure. He socks them away in a box by his desk. When he refers to these journals, the random phrases begin a dialogue, often with each other, always with him. Flipping through these small journals, Stafford discovers clusters of fragments that suggest organizing thoughts and inspire his poems, picture books, essays, and novels.

—Sometimes the only door into certain parts of you may be available in a wild place.

—Someone said, "No two siblings grow up in the same family."

—Dream sentence: "The air is not open to you, until you open it."

—Wall plaque: "This life is a test and only a test. If it were not a test, you would have been given specific instructions on where to go and what to do."

Stafford arrived at a life crossroads when a friend challenged him to reevaluate his dependence on journal keeping: "When you wake up tomorrow, if there is something you want to do, either do it, or decide not to do it. But don't travel sideways by writing about a character who does what you want." Stafford handed over his notebook. When the friend returned the journal a month later, Stafford reread it and was amazed to find numerous lectures to himself about how to cope with unhappiness. The lesson he draws from this experience as a writer is to use the journal principally for gathering empirical evidence.

Stafford's journal-keeping habit now reigns everywhere — in computer files, on 3-by-5 index cards scattered throughout his writing files, and, of course, in his heart pocket books. It's a continual, seamless process, one he tailors to fit personal literary and academic purposes.

For a while, Stafford experimented capturing wispy dream messages in a night-table notebook. Trying to learn from Dorothy Wordsworth's practice, every night Stafford wrote one sentence about what was happening around him, then one sentence about what was happening inside his heart. "She had such a wonderful way of putting the two perspectives together," he says. In various journals, Stafford also blends both perspectives. Gathering material and writing it down in his journal is for Stafford "like having a meal — it's feasting on the language of the world." He also listens to his heart.

"Emerson pointed out that in all works of genius, we recognize our own neglected thoughts." What this says to writers, says Stafford, is to pay attention to inner musings and give thoughts the chance to avoid neglect. "Give yourself the constant permission to jot a note to your future, a note that could become your own work of genius."

Kim Stafford's books include

We Got Here Together
Wind on the Waves
Entering the Grove
Having Everything Right: Essays of Place
Lochsa Road: A Pilgrim in the West
A Thousand Friends of Rain

The Interview

I would date serious journal keeping to my junior English teacher, Miss Scholastica Murty. Her friends called her Scully, and she was a genius. Certain teachers are helpless in the face of their own love of literature and stories, and she was one who would perch on her toes out of excitement before us as she read. She had us keep journals and she would write back comments, sometimes longer than the entries we wrote, but often just short appreciative remarks: "I like this ever so much." She was very sweet, but strangely tough-minded at the same time, and not to be schooled by the world to abandon inner emotional experience and feelings and thoughts and dreams. She was an inspiration to me, and I've kept a journal ever since her class.

The beginning of journal keeping, though, was my parents' habit. When we were little kids they wrote down things we said in a book called "Lost Words." My parents were both teachers, and writing down our words was their habit of being alert to language.

My grandmother kept a journal called "The New Life" that she started on her wedding day in June 1902. She sealed it shut with sealing wax, and wrote on the outside "sealed until finished," meaning until her life was finished. Her private thoughts are rich and wonderful: "This then is to be the Day of Days . . ."

I urge parents to have a book by the dining room table and every night jot down some of the things the kids have said. We all begin as geniuses, discovering what language can be. We all have literary heritage. Anyone could be the jaybird of the family.

Heart Pocket Books

I make my own journals, sewing together little books that fit in my pocket that I call "heart pocket books." I use a thread with beeswax so that it has a nice aroma every time I get it out. Fairly frequently they go through the wash so I use a waterproof ink. They get kind of fuzzy that way, but they're still legible.

I'll be in a meeting or waiting for the bus, and out of boredom or silence rich things from earlier in the day well up, things I've suppressed because I'm such a good citizen and I'm hurrying from place to place and trying to please many people. Unintentionally I've repressed the great rich abundance of life. When I have this book handy, though, I don't have to make the decision—is this important enough to write down or do I have the time to write this down? It's "Oh, I'll jot that down."

Sometimes during conversation a person will make an unintentional poetic discovery and I want to harvest their, I guess you could say, "mistake" in language. I whip out my heart pocket book and write it down. Recently someone asked if I would come and present a workshop on the "Thriller Slash Horror Book," and I loved the use of the word "slash" in that particular context. I didn't want it to get away.

A journalist once told me that being a reporter is having a passport to all of human life. It's your job to inquire, to interview, to examine things. My journal is that kind of passport. Writing things down makes us smarter, or rather, makes us better able to participate in the genius of the world.

Life in Layers

I think that by keeping a journal my life happens twice. Even if I don't go back to the journal, I have a better chance of remembering observations or emotional events having written them down. Because I'm in the habit of translating events into language as a regular part of daily experience, I feel like I'm having a life with several layers.

I think we could make the connection that any kind of journal keeping is preserving the multiple voices of the self. There's a kind of assumption that we are to have achieved a balanced view by the time we enter into discourse with others, but in the journal one can be extravagant in many different directions without fear of being thought foolish.

Seamless Process

I don't set aside any special time for journal writing. There are so many opportunities, and with the heart pocket book so convenient, to me it's continual.

Letter writing is another kind of journal keeping. When you write about something that's important to you and send this to someone to whom you are important, that's a magic formula.

It's like having a very welcoming teacher who will not say, "I don't understand what you're saying . . . maybe you should put it in this form." Rather, it's a friend saying, "How wonderful, tell me more about that . . . I'm so eager to hear anything you send."

I keep a journal of certain projects I'm working on. I have a separate journal for a novel I'm writing. Sometimes I'll have things in my heart pocket book and I transfer them to that journal.

I keep a journal on my computer that's my most private of all. When I'm having a time of emotional learning I take a half hour and cluster ideas. At certain times I've had a dream journal, which I keep by my bed.

I kept what I call my Dorothy Wordsworth journal for a while, trying to learn from her way. Every night I would write one sentence about what was happening outside in the world, and then one sentence about what was happening inside my heart. She had such a wonderful way of putting two perspectives together. "William not home; foxgloves just coming into bloom."

Audience and Privacy

When I write in my journal, it's like having a meal. It's delicious fragments; it's feasting on the language of the world. And what is the audience for a meal? I consider my journal completely private and completely safe. If someone else were to read it, well, it could be at their peril. I never have any feeling of not saying what I want to say. The solution to privacy is not in the journal, but in some kind of understanding within the household.

There is a heartless proverb, but I think it's related. When students tell me about reading their poems to friends and getting back comments of complaint or judgment, I tell them, "Judge your friends by your poems, not your poems by your friends. If they don't like your poems, well, that's too bad."

One way to have the journal experience and be completely

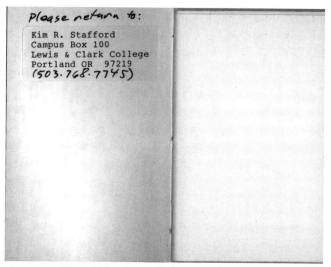

Please return to:

Kim R. Stafford
Campus Box 100
Lewis & Clark College
Portland OR   97219
(503.768.7745)

One of Kim Stafford's heart pocket books

safe at the same time would be to write and burn, or write and discard, or write and hide.

I took a pen name for a year, a woman's name because I wanted complete privacy when I wrote and published. In this experiment, for example, I thought I could tell all of the family stories that otherwise would be dangerous. So this woman writer wrote these stories with complete freedom for a year. At the end of the year I thought, well, that was a good experience, but it has fulfilled it's purpose. The difficulty of trying to tell the truth without hurting others is a very good difficulty. Complete freedom where no one knows and no one cares is not a world I choose.

Secrets Ready to Be Told

The first stage of telling all in the journal is to find the part of the truth that you can tell people. I tell my students, "Write the secrets you are ready to tell." Somewhere within the text of an angry letter or a secret story is a sentence that holds your truth. Recognize the whole secret, and tell the ready part. That's why I like this formulation of a secret you are ready to tell, but I caution students not to tell that secret if they are not ready. I don't want to push anyone into thinking they're an incomplete human being if there are things they are afraid to tell. The boundary shifts daily between what you are not and what you are ready to tell.

I'm thinking of a time in class when I had a student who wrote and shared a very revealing piece, and then was so frightened she didn't share anything for the rest of the term. She didn't yet know how to make it safe for herself within her writing. That takes experience.

Working with Dreams

One of the peaks of creativity is grades three and four. When I visit an elementary class and ask how many people had a dream last night, it's everybody, and they're all excited about sharing. So often the dream is concocted in a language by the mind that it doesn't really reveal itself until you are writing it down. I'm not talking about interpreting, just putting it into language so that it has a second chance to be understood.

One thing I've done with kids and journals is to have them write down a dream, then translate it into something that could happen in real life. They create a short story from a dream. One boy's dream was about a bull chasing him around the house. When he translated it into a story he wrote about his dad chasing him. It's a very innocent kind of psychoanalysis, but to the child it's just a story of his father chasing him and bellowing. I don't have to say your dad is the bull. I just say tell this dream in a way that could actually happen.

Journal as Salvation

I made a vow to myself, some years ago when I became a college administrator, that every memo I had to write would include a paragraph that I wanted to write. My journal always has some delicious thing I can put into a memo, no matter how formal. This is salvation in professional life. I find myself doing this in letters, too.

When I left school, I thought I would be totally free with no one else to give me assignments. But in my writing life there are assignments from the world: write a speech, write a column, write an essay about this or that. Instead of staring at a blank page or a blank computer screen, I begin flipping through my notebooks, and inevitably a cluster of fragments that was taken down randomly becomes susceptible to some organizing thought.

It seems a magic process. Instead of starting with nothing, I find in my journal the seeds of whatever garden I want to grow, whether it's a poem, speech, essay or story.

Journal by Example

Teachers often work too hard. They think they have to be in charge of all the learning, and that if they set an activity in motion where the kids are making their own decisions then the teacher has committed a white collar crime. They think they must be cheating if the students are doing the work. When I'm a guest in a classroom I try not to talk about writing, but to do it. My rule for myself is that I always write with the students. If I exude concentration, that's the best I can do. I don't have any rules for the students, just invitations and encouragement. Writing is a subversive and democratically possible activity. The experience of writing is the proof of its own importance. Writing is the teacher.

Often I will start out by reading something aloud or asking a question. Conversation starts, and all of a sudden there's a lot more people wanting to say something than there is time to speak. That's the time to turn conversation into writing. Writing is hands-on conversation. It's hands-on thinking.

Gretchen Will Mayo

"My Footprint on the Path"

Gretchen Will Mayo, age 7

For many writers there is nothing more terrifying than facing the blank page. A recent, self-imposed change in her creative life left author/illustrator Gretchen Will Mayo without a focus. Rather than feeling stuck or panicked, she turned anew to writing in her journal to answer the question: What next? Now, hundreds of pages of free writing and several volumes of observational journals later, Mayo is beginning to see patterns emerging from research into her family history and cultural background.

From the days of early childhood, Mayo has been guided by an intensely inquisitive nature and a deep love of stories. She grew up in Centerville, Ohio, where mound-building Indians had once lived. As a child she found shards of pottery, arrow-heads, and grinding stones, artifacts that ignited her curiosity. An avid reader of folktales from around the world, she wondered where she could find stories about the Indians. For a long time, her question remained unanswered, a strand in a braid that would eventually come back to her and be woven into the pattern of a successful writing career.

Years later while camping out under the stars with her husband and three little girls, Mayo told stories about the heavenly bodies of light. Curious about sky stories for children, but finding none that had originated on this continent, Mayo combed university libraries searching for Native American star stories. Attracted to the ethnological studies published by the U.S. Government, she came to realize that Indians had not been using a written language at the time explorers and settlers were discovering the New World and recording their journeys. At the same time she became aware of the authenticity issue: stories written with good intentions, but seen through the lens of another culture, needed to be traced to their earliest sources and verified by experts. After four years of painstaking research, Mayo published *Star Tales*, her first volume of Native American stories. In the years that followed, she retold and illustrated many Native American tales, including coyote and rabbit versions of trickster tales, and sky and earthmaker tales, always taking care to authenticate her material.

Acutely aware that Indian voices were silent in the world of children's literature, Mayo brought together Wisconsin tribal leaders to form Woodland Writers. Directing writing retreats, critiquing manuscripts, and encouraging and mentoring American Indians, Mayo shared her hard-earned experience in publishing. As she worked with Native American writers, she became uncomfortable telling their stories. "It's risky business to work with stories that come from other cultures, especially when they have roots deep into a spiritual life," she says. "And that's true of American Indian stories."

With no idea of what to write or illustrate next, Mayo let go of American Indian material. Had it not been for her journal, her richly creative life could have become a blank page. To keep going she explored areas that captured her intellectual curiosity, but now through the lens of her own Irish heritage. Partly to dig into her Irish-German roots as well as to satisfy another lifelong curiosity, Mayo wrote a family history. She gathered information and attended Irish festivals, all the while making notes and doodling with snippets of Celtic art designs. Because her creativity is stimulated by doing artwork with her hands, Mayo decorated furniture and crafted bowls and border designs.

For two years Mayo's own voice in the world of children's publishing was silent. By choice, she has set off on a different path. Following her faithful spirit guide — curiosity — she went inward to find her own stories. In her journal she collected observations and combined them with reflections about her inner life. She placed her wishes, dreams and sorrows on the pages of her journal to allow them to "mingle with the universe and become part of a wholeness rather than a divider" in her life. Now, with the sales of short stories and nonfiction for children based on her Irish heritage, Gretchen Will Mayo has established a fresh pathway in her writing career.

Gretchen Will Mayo's books include

That Tricky Coyote
Meet Tricky Coyote
Star Tales: North American Indian Stories About the Stars
Earthmaker's Tales: North American Indian Stories About Earth
  Happenings
Big Trouble for Tricky Rabbit
Whale Brother

The Interview

Keeping a diary was dangerous in the house where I grew up. I had three curious younger brothers who weren't above pulling out pages of my locked diary with tweezers. One time they sold some pages for five cents to a neighbor. So I stopped keeping one. Later, in my teens, I took to writing long descriptive letters to relatives and friends. In college I wrote home the same kinds of letters. When I was the mother of three toddlers and feeling as though I was losing a sense of myself, I began to pour out my heart into my journals. Reading them now, it hurts to see how much self-confidence I had lost.

Paying Attention

Journal writing is my way of paying attention and being a witness as events and places unfold. In one journal I keep daily observations about my world, my reactions to external events and memories. This "life journal" says a lot about family events, wildlife, the seasons, nature, and relationships. I like discovering patterns through my observations of people, places, animals, and nature. The organic nature of my spiritual life becomes quite clear.

I share these journals with my children because they reveal not only my era but also parts of me that they may not know. My father died early with much unfinished business. My mother dislikes writing letters or journals and is very closed about her own life. I've had a lifelong curiosity about these two important people. I'm trying to change the pattern for the sake of my own children.

Another running journal is for free-writing anything that happens to creep out of my subconscious—all the shadowy things I wouldn't dare say to most people. It is clearly marked IN CASE OF MY DEMISE, BURN THIS! Some of this free writing is nothing but trash, and I have to suck in my breath when I read over it later. It's quite embarrassing, really. But along with the trash lie important ideas that have changed the way I feel about some matters and also a few good ideas for books.

This journal is sloppy and exhibits no regard for punctuation, sentence structure, or logic and reads like a stream-of-consciousness. It's almost dreamlike and is often hard to follow. In it I often try to work out problems that arise in my creative process.

A Delicate Balance

I find that if I let my subconscious speak its mind first thing in the morning, it leaves me feeling unburdened and freer to create. However, free writing and recording observations in my life journal feel so good that they can seduce me away from the other things that bring me creative satisfaction but require real effort. There have been times when I've been aware that my journal writing was skimming off the best part of me, that after pouring myself into a journal my creative impulses weren't fresh anymore that day. I have to be careful not to fall into the trap of giving too much of myself—too much time and energy—to journaling. I used to let myself go at free writing until I was finished. If there's something really juicy going on I will continue for longer than my usual thirty minutes. When I have things on the plate for the day, I try to discipline myself and not let journaling take over entirely.

Discovering Treasures

When my creative work-in-progress presents a problem I free-write to allow my subconscious to give me ideas that might otherwise lay buried. This type of journaling often includes rapid-fire list making. For example, when trying to get Rabbit out of a fix, I may free write about his options and their consequences. If a female character needs a disguise, I'll get into her thought process and write out what I would do in her situation. This kind of journaling energy has given me treasures. The situations in my journals become the strengths and weaknesses of my characters. The tensions in stories derive from opposing forces described or hinted at on the pages of my journals. And my journals are filled with small details that make my stories rich.

Prayer Wheel, Footprint, and Playground

I consider my free-writing journal a prayer wheel, a place where anything I write is accepted, especially my deepest thoughts. I've always imagined a prayer wheel as the place to put my wishes, dreams, and sorrows, a place for them to mingle into the universe and became part of a wholeness rather than a divider in my life. I find this aspect of it very healing. My daily observation journal is my footprint on the path. I believe we are all on a journey, that's what life is. And we are always in a different place. When you write you make a marker, a record of where you've been in your life. I don't keep a separate notebook for each book I write, but I keep messes of papers. I like to reuse things so I cut manila envelopes that come to me in the mail and make a file where I store clippings or notes. When the first one gets too fat, I label it and start another. If I get stuck, I pull out a snippet from the envelope and free-write about it. I might free-write as my character. Now journaling becomes a playground for my creative work.

Wilderness Journal

My daughter Ann works as a national park ranger on Isle Royale in Lake Superior. When the lake is iced-in she works in Ely, Minnesota, which is the entryway to the boundary waters. I had gone up to visit her there in January when there were three feet of snow and temperatures in the minus forties. We snuggled in our down blankets and wrote in our journals. We started reading things to each other. First we laughed. Then we cried. We said "You know what we ought to do? We should journal for each other."

Three stages of "Boy Who Shot the Star," from *Star Tales*

For my birthday Ann gave me a small spiral-bound book. We had to make it small so she could carry it when she is out in the wilds, backpacking or canoeing. I was the first to make entries. Then I sent it to her. Ann took it along on a six-week canoe trip she made with a friend in the boundary waters. So far we've exchanged the journal three times. It's a wonderful way to communicate, especially because she's often completely out of touch for weeks or even months. This way we both have a record of our thoughts and I get to keep up with her as her experiences and perceptions accumulate.

Ann also writes letters when she is in the wilderness, and we keep them for her so they aren't destroyed. The letters are another form of journal keeping. With my daughter in New York, it's E-mail. My daughter in Denver prefers the telephone.

Journal Phases

Like many other people I go through phases. For years I didn't keep formal journals, but wrote letters and notes to myself. In the last ten years I've been more intentional and organized about keeping my thoughts and observations. Since then I've written over 2,000 pages of free writing and ten daily observational journals.

I'm really picky about my journals now. First, they must be spiral books so that the pages lie flat. Second, my free writing journal must have lines so I'm not distracted by trying to write straight. It is cheaper than my other journal because I want it to feel less precious, disposable. My daily observations journal definitely must not have lines. That leaves me free to sketch. This journal must have thick paper so that I can't see any evidence of writing from the other side of the page.

I used to ignore the urge to "throw up" on paper. I only wrote nice stuff. I still write the nice stuff in a separate journal, but now I give vent to the harsh and cloudy thoughts. By getting out my shadowy, "in your face" self, I find I can leave them behind.

Over the years I've used my journal to explore and carefully examine my own basic assumptions. I've come to believe that we all see the world and other people through the colored lens of our own cultural upbringing. Understanding and compassion will grow only if I work to get beyond those imposed assumptions. Journal writing is a safe place to expose my own inner thoughts to the light and work on them.

Words of Wisdom

If you want to keep a journal, push yourself to make more than a list of the day's events. Write about your feelings and the details that capture your attention. Through this kind of journal writing you will become more aware of your own passions and the swirling world around you, and you'll come to better understand how and why things happen. Practice paying attention, practice stringing words together, and play with ideas.

Acknowledgments

Permission to reprint copyrighted material included in *Speaking of Journals* is gratefully acknowledged to the following:

Richard Ammon, journal entry. Copyright © 1999 by Richard Ammon.

Jim Arnosky, sketches. Copyright © 1999 by Jim Arnosky.

Barbara Bash, journal entry with sketches. Copyright © 1999 by Barbara Bash.

Marion Dane Bauer, letter. Copyright © 1999 by Marion Dane Bauer.

Lynne Cherry, sketches. Copyright © 1999 by Lynne Cherry.

Jennifer Owings Dewey, sketches. Copyright © 1999 by Jennifer Owings Dewey.

Jack Gantos, journal entry. Copyright © 1999 by Jack Gantos.

Patricia Lee Gauch, journal entry. Copyright © 1999 by Patricia Lee Gauch.

Jean Craighead George, journal entries and sketches. Copyright © 1999 by Jean Craighead George.

James Cross Giblin, journal entries. Copyright © 1999 by James Cross Giblin.

David Harrison, journal entries. Copyright © 1999 by David Harrison.

Sara Holbrook, poems: "Private Parts," from *The Dog Ate My Homework.* Copyright © 1996 by Sara Holbrook; "May I Be Excused?" from *Nothing's the End of the World.* Copyright © 1995 by Sara Holbrook; "The Trip to the Zoo" from *Which Way to the Dragon?* Copyright © 1996 by Sara Holbrook. Jjournal entries. Copyright © 1999 by Sara Holbrook.

Kathleen Krull, journal entries. Copyright © 1999 by Kathleen Krull.

Mary E. Lyons, journal entries. Copyright © 1999 by Mary E. Lyons.

Judith Logan Lehne, journal entries. Copyright © 1999 by Judith Logan Lehne.

Gretchen Will Mayo, sketches. Copyright © 1999 by Gretchen Will Mayo.

Mary Jane Miller, journal entries. Copyright © 1999 by Mary Jane Miller.

Naomi Shihab Nye, journal entries. Copyright © 1999 by Naomi Shihab Nye.

Graham Salisbury, journal entry. Copyright © 1999 by Graham Salisbury.

Eileen Spinelli, journal entries. Copyright © 1999 by Eileen Spinelli.

Kim Stafford, journal entries. Copyright © 1999 by by Kim Stafford.

Stephen Trimble, journal entries. Copyright © 1999 by Stephen Trimble.

Rich Wallace, journal entries. Copyright © 1999 by Rich Wallace.

Terry Tempest Williams, journal entries. Copyright © 1999 by Terry Tempest Williams.